HILLEBRANDT

&

BEAR DOG

BONE & LORAINE NOVEL #11

By

KEN FARMER

Cover By:
K. R. FARMER

ISBN - 979-8-88862-985-7
Timber Creek Press
Imprint of Timber Creek Productions, LLC
312 N. Commerce St.
Gainesville, Texas 76240
Facebook Book Page:
https://www.facebook.com/ken.storyteller/
Ken's email: pagact@yahoo.com

ACKNOWLEDGMENT

The author gratefully acknowledges Lt. Colonel Clyde DeLoach, USMC (Ret.), Terry D. Heflin - retired English Professor at Tarrant County College and author, Cynthia Morast-Foster, teacher, Colleen Hlavac - author, and retired police officer James Bryan, retired Dallas PD, for their invaluable help in proofing, beta reading, and editing this novel.

This novel is a work of fiction...except the parts that aren't. Names, characters, places, and incidents are either the products of the author's imagination or are used fictitiously. Any resemblance to actual persons, living or dead, business establishments, events, or locales is entirely coincidental, except where they aren't.

TIMBER CREEK PRESS

CHAPTER ONE

NORTH TEXAS

"Creek's up a mite, Sugar Babe...Think we'll have to wait a day or two to cross this puppy."

Loraine looked left to the north then back to Bone. "That iron bridge that crosses this creek to get to Gainesville is completely underwater...except for those iron beams over the top."

"Looks kinda like when this creek flooded in 1981...before we got caught in that time portal that sent us to 1898."

"The flood that washed Sissy, the elephant, from the Frank Buck Zoo in Gainesville...and carried her downstream?"

Bone nodded. "Yep, found her two days later when the water went down. She had wedged herself between two trees...Kept her trunk above the water to breathe...Poor thing was so traumatized by being underwater for all that time, they couldn't bathe her for over twenty years."

"She at that sanctuary in Tennessee now, or in 2018?...Uh, well, guess it's 2022 there."

"Uh-huh."

Bone and Loraine sat their horses on a high bank above the Elm Fork of the Trinity River watching the result of an overnight ten-inch rain.

HILDEBRANDT & BEAR DOG

The creek was up over thirty feet as it rolled and churned its way toward the Trinity River which eventually flowed into the Gulf of Mexico.

The big, black, half-wolf, Bear Dog...that actually belonged to Silke Justice...sat on the ground beside Bone's seventeen-hand, black, half-Friesian gelding, Hildebrandt, as they watched the boiling muddy water heading south below them.

Loraine leaned her forearms on the top of her saddlehorn. Her horse was a bright red copper sorrel, blaze-face, quarter-horse mare she named Sweet Face.

"What do you want to do, then, Bone?"

He twisted in his saddle to look back at her. "Guess we'll have to go back to Fiona an'...Whoa!"

The bank abruptly sloughed off, plunging him, Hildebrandt, and Bear Dog into the maelstrom below.

"Get back, Babe, back!"

Loraine backed Sweet Face quickly away from the unstable bank as they disappeared into the muddy flood.

She turned the mare to the side. "Bone! Bone!...Oh, God!"

Loraine trotted Sweet Face along the bank downstream trying to catch sight of her husband, Hildebrandt, and Bear Dog.

Bone instinctively grabbed for the hemp rope tied securely to the front saddle string on the right side of his saddle. He managed to grasp it with his left hand as the current tumbled and swept him and the massive horse downstream.

The fifteen-hundred pound horse valiantly struck out for the opposite bank almost a hundred feet away. His legs churned fiercely against the swift current as he was periodically pulled under the surface.

He dragged Bone along with him as they were swept downstream together toward the mighty Trinity at Dallas, over seventy miles away. Several uprooted trees, caught in the flood, narrowly missed them.

The giant wolf-dog was also tumbled over and over by the tumult—he too, would be pulled under only to struggle until his head poked back above the water where he would take a breath.

Loraine and Sweet Face kept pace with the speed of the water, occasionally catching a glimpse of Hildebrandt's head popping to the top with Bone in tow as they were swept along like a child's toy.

Bone managed to hook his right arm through the loops of the rope to add to the steel-like grip of his left. They were at the mercy of the churning flood waters. *Hope I tied this sucker on tight.*

When Hildebrandt managed to get his head above the foaming water, Bone would too. He grabbed several quick breaths knowing they would be jerked quickly back under.

Hang on, Bone, hang on. Let the big guy do his thing...Trust 'im. He felt Hildebrandt hit the top of a sandbar with his front feet, then they were swept past it. His lungs began to burn and he could no longer feel the rope in his hand, but he knew it was there. *They'll have to prise my fingers off, if we're ever found.*

Loraine was forced away from the creek bank to go around a large copse of cedar, shinnery, post oak, and other brush too thick to ride through.

When she got around it and back to the swollen creek, she couldn't see any sign of Bone, Hildebrandt, or Bear Dog. Loraine looked up and down the creek trying to see any sign—nothing.

She turned Sweet Face and galloped her downstream thinking it took longer to go around those trees than she thought.

Loraine stopped on a rise and could see almost a half-mile downstream from her vantage point on the other side. She scanned both banks—again, nothing.

She, Bone, and Bear Dog were on the way back to Gainesville after visiting with former Sheriff Mason Flynn and his wife, Deputy US Marshal Fiona Miller Flynn at their ranch on the western side of Cooke County.

They had to cross the Elm Fork of the Trinity on the west side of Gainesville to get back to Faye Skean's Boarding House just past downtown.

He and Loraine had lived there since being transported here in 1898 from 2018 through an ancient Native American portal in a cave near what is now Possum Kingdom Lake in Palo Pinto County.

Mason Flynn, former sheriff of Clay County, had gotten a telegram that the new sheriff that replaced him, James (Jip) Coltrane, had gone missing under mysterious circumstances. He needed Bone and Loraine to see if they could track him down.

Hildebrandt continued to struggle against the powerful flood water's current. Bone admired the strength and perseverance of his half-Friesian and half-American Saddlebred gelding. *Big guy's gotta lotta heart.*

They came to the surface again, just in time for Bone as he had been struck in the head by a thigh-thick limb in the swirling water, and knocked briefly unconscious. He shook his head to clear the water from his eyes and could see the east bank of the swollen creek only twenty feet away—Hildebrant could, too.

The mighty horse surged with a Herculean effort churning his legs toward the safety of the bank. His steel-shod feet touched bottom briefly, losing purchase twice, then after what seemed like an eternity to Bone, managed to get firmer footing and struggled up the bank—they were over ten miles from where they fell in.

HILDEBRANDT & BEAR DOG

The valiant animal collapsed on dry land, only his back feet touched the edge of the swirling water. Bone pulled himself forward and lay prone beside Hildebrandt—he too, was totally exhausted.

The big horse shuddered and convulsed as he coughed up muddy water. His heaving sides rose and fell rapidly as the fatigued animal tried to take enough air into his starved lungs.

Bone weakly managed to get his arm over Hildebrandt's neck. "Thank you, Boy, thank you."

He managed to pull his knees up where he could crouch next to the brave totally fagged out animal's head. Bone got an arm under it and cradled it in his lap so he could whisper in Hildebrandt's ear.

"Come on, Son, stay with me, stay with me...You made it. We're safe."

After a long moment, Hildebrandt moaned and grunted, then raised his head and rolled to his knees. He struggled to push himself up front first like horses do, then he followed with his hindquarters until he was standing shakily on all fours. They were spread out almost like a foal would stand—wobbling, trying to find his balance.

His sides still heaved as his muscles quivered and shook from the massive effort of the last hour.

Bone also managed to slowly stand and stroke the gallant horse's face, placing his forehead against his still damp neck.

Hildebrandt had a white star just above and between his eyes, the only color, other than black, on his body—he liked for Bone to rub on top of the mark and hung his head in pleasure.

Bone looked around as Hildebrandt slowly recuperated. He spied Bear Dog a little further down the bank.

The big wolf-dog laid like a rag doll at the edge of the swirling water.

"Bear Dog!...Bear Dog!"

The mass stirred and the two-hundred pound animal lifted his head at Bone's voice. He managed to roll over and crawled toward the big man on his belly, inching forward a little at a time.

Bone was not able to walk yet, but he dropped back down to his knees and crawled to meet his loyal friend.

Hildebrandt turned and followed him, staggering a little a couple of times.

They reached the big wolf-dog almost at the same time. Hildebrandt reached down with his nose and nudged Bear Dog.

They almost looked like a matched pair as both coal-black animals had a single white mark in the middle of their foreheads—there was a special bond between them and Bone.

The only color difference was that Bear Dog had bright blue eyes while Hildebrandt's were a soft, limpid, golden-brown.

Bear Dog licked Bone's hand, then Hildebrandt's nose. The big horse returned the affection by twitching his upper lip and softly nibbling the wolf-dog's head as he nuzzled him.

Bone looked around again, back at the dirty flood waters, then at his two companions as he frowned.

"Well, don't rightly know where we are Boys...Know who you are, but more importantly...don't rightly know who I am, either."

Three miles back upstream, Loraine sat slumped and dejected in her saddle, tears streamed down her face as she stared blankly at the muddy, flooded creek.

§§§

CHAPTER TWO

NORTH TEXAS

"This is really strange, boys...know who you are..." He shook his head. "...but no idea in hell who I am." Bone looked around at the bucolic, rolling hills with scattered cottonwood, sweet gum, and post oaks. "Or where we are."

There were larger hardwoods, pin oaks, pecan, and hickory along the flooded creek.

Bone could feel a weight on his hip. He looked, and then reached down, unsnapped the strap, and pulled a stainless steel Smith & Wesson .50 caliber handgun from the scabbard.

"What the heck?" He turned it over and hefted it. "Um...Sucker's heavy. What am I carryin' this for?" He noticed the white carving that looked like a bone inset in both sides of the grip. "Huh?...That's interesting."

Bone looked down at Bear Dog. "Guess if you know, you ain't tellin'."

Woof.

"What I thought." He looked at the holster again. "Probably a good thing this was strapped in while that creek was playin' with us...Wish I had something dry, should clean this before it starts rustin'...Have to wait, I guess."

HILDEBRANDT & BEAR DOG

Hildebrandt had recovered enough he was cropping some of the fresh prairie grass under his feet.

Bone stepped over to him, unstrapped his girth and pulled the saddle and blanket from his back.

"Better hang this on a limb, Big Guy, let it dry. Wet saddle blanket an' saddle will give you galls in a heartbeat...probably me too."

He found a low, reasonably horizontal, limb on a white oak strong enough to hold the water-soaked saddle and blanket and hung them on it. Bone unfolded the Navajo wool saddle blanket first so it would dry quicker.

He looked to see what was in his saddlebags after taking his shirt off and hanging it on another limb. Bone finally got his wet boots off and stuck each one on a branch he'd trimmed the end and leaves from to dry, too.

Among some other things in the bags, there was a packet of jerky wrapped in oiled paper. Water had still gotten in, but would soon dry away if he unwrapped it and spread the tough, dried beef out on a rock.

He glanced at Bear Dog laying beside him where he was inspecting the contents of the bag. "Should be all right, Bear Dog, can't hardly hurt jerky unless you let it get moldy...'Course can always scrape it off with a knife, that happens."

Bone felt of his jean's pocket. "Whew! Pocket knife's still there...Gibb's rule number 9...'Never go anywhere without a knife'."

He reached in, took it out, and hit the button to unfold the drop-point, tactical combat, razor-sharp knife blade. It was made of stainless steel, plus, coated with a black rust and stain preventative.

Bone pulled some of the tall prairie grass and rubbed the big horse's back to dry ii where the saddle had set. Hildebrandt nickered his pleasure and kept grazing, but only for a moment.

He noticed an almost bare spot, walked over, promptly laid down and rolled back and forth several times. Hildebrandt got to his feet and violently shook, sending tiny pieces of grass and sand up in a cloud from his hair.

Bone facetiously frowned. "Just have a bath an' right off you gotta roll in the dirt."

Loraine continued to ride up and down the creek bank, frantically looking for any sign. She had no way to know Bone, Hildebrandt, and Bear Dog had moved away from the rushing water on the other side behind a hill, out of sight of the creek.

She had been desperately searching for over three hours. Her face was drawn and showed dried tear streaks on both cheeks along with her bloodshot eyes.

Sweet Face was tiring and occasionally stumbling before Loraine finally stopped. Once again she stared blankly at the muddy, flooded creek.

"Oh, Bone, why? Why did it have to be you?...Why did that bank have to give away right when we rode up?"

Loraine turned the fatigued mare and headed back to Fiona and Mason's ranch at a walk. She slumped in the saddle with her chin on her chest as Sweet Face shuffled back to the west—she knew the mare knew the way. They had five miles to cover.

Three hours later, Loraine tied Sweet Face to the peeled cedar hitching rail in front of the rambling, native stone ranch house.

Loraine slowly walked up the flagstone path to the stoop, turned and dropped heavily to the top step. She leaned over with her face cupped in both hands and let the tears gush forth. Her body shook with sobs as she tried to catch her breath.

Fiona and Mason burst out the screen door, letting it slam behind them with a bang.

Fiona rushed forward where Loraine sat. "Loraine! My, God, what's wrong, Honey? We heard you ride up...What's happened?" She looked up and only saw Sweet Face. "Where's Bone?"

Loraine turned to the older woman and buried her face in her bosom when Fiona sat down beside her. She choked and jerked as she tried to talk. Nothing would come out.

Mason sat on the other side and looked at Fiona. "Something's happened to Bone."

Fiona nodded and stroked Loraine's black hair in an effort to calm her.

Loraine held most of her emotions in check on the ride back, but now the walls came down like Jericho as Fiona held her.

After a moment, she caught her breath. "He's gone, Fiona, he's gone."

Fiona looked over at Mason, then back down at Loraine. "What do you mean, Loraine? Gone where?"

She took a deep breath, then another before leaning back to look at Fiona with her tear-filled, red-rimmed eyes. "Bone...Hildebrandt an' Bear Dog...They all...all fell in Elm Creek when the...the flood collapsed...collapsed the bank where...where they were." She took another breath. "They...they disappeared in that...awful muddy water as...it carried them...them downstream."

Fiona hugged her. "Oh, Honey...Don't worry...We'll find them. I promise...They'll be all right. We all know Bone...He's not about to let any flood take him...Trust me."

Loraine leaned back again. "I searched downstream for miles...lookin'...lookin' for...for any sign." She shook her head. "Nothin'."

Mason got to his feet. "I'll go saddle the horses." He looked out at Loraine's exhausted mare. "And another for Loraine. Sweet Face is too fagged out to ride for at least a day or so."

Fiona nodded at her husband.

He strode down the walk, untied Sweet Face and led her to the barn.

Fiona put her hands on both Loraine's shoulders and held her out at arms length. "We'll find him, Honey. I promise...Not going to lose my only great-grandson." She forced a smile. "Don't tell him I said so...Now come inside and wash up. You need to eat something before we head out."

Loraine pursed her lips. "Not sure I can, Fiona."

"You can...an' will."

They got to their feet and Fiona led her inside.

Charlotte's nanny, a young Chickasaw woman named, *Hashi Lakna'*, or Yellow Moon, approached as they headed to the kitchen. "You need Yellow Moon fix food, Miz Fiona?"

The Chickasaw woman was a niece of the tribal Shaman *Anompoli Lawa,* or He Who Talks to Many, and was an acolyte of the Hatchet Woman Clan, a female warrior clan of the Chickasaw.

Silke Justice had been inducted as an honorary member into the clan several years ago for tracking down and eliminating an outlaw gang harassing the Chickasaw.

"No, it's all right, Yellow Moon, I can handle it...We'll be gone for the rest of the afternoon. You can tell Charlotte when she wakes up from her nap."

Bone and Bear Dog leaned against the gray bole of a big cottonwood munching on jerky while Hildebrandt continued to graze only ten yards away.

"Feelin' better, Buddy?"

"Woof." He reached out with a paw and laid it on Bone's thigh.

He handed the wolf-dog another piece of jerky and he swallowed it whole.

"You could chew it, first, you know."

Bear Dog looked at him with his grin.

Bone studied the sky for a long moment and finally shook his head. "Another thing I can't figure out, in addition to who I am an' where we are..." He looked up at the clear blue sky again. "...is maybe when are we...Haven't seen a contrail all afternoon...not one." Bone looked down at Bear Dog. "Now, that's odd, idn't it?"

The big animal looked back at Bone and cocked his head to the right.

§§§

CHAPTER THREE

NORTH TEXAS

Loraine, Fiona, and Mason trotted their horses east toward Gainesville and the Elm Fork of the Trinity.

"When do you think that creek will be down enough we can cross to the other side on the bridge at the edge of Gainesville?...Assumin' it's still there."

Loraine glanced over at Fiona. "Had a worse flood in 1981, before Bone and I were transported here through that portal...Went down in two days."

"How many inches of rain did you get then?"

"That one was seventeen inches in a twenty-four hour period. A lot of downtown had almost two-feet of water."

Mason shook his head. "Must have a bit of a drainage problem."

"You could say...They started fixing the problem around the year 2000 or so."

Fiona grimaced. "Doesn't help much now, though."

Loraine shook her head. "No."

"The only good thing is, we only got ten inches or so...If we can't find them this afternoon, we can go into Gainesville soon as we can cross, get Silke, Bodie, and them to help."

Loraine took a deep breath. "They would help now...if they knew."

"They would...Were they expectin' ya'll back today?"

"Not really, Mason. You know Bone. Always says, 'be back when we're back'."

Fiona shifted her saddle back to the center on her red and white paint mule, Spot. "Uh-huh...Either that or 'look for us when you see us comin'."

"That's my Bone."

Fiona glanced around the rolling grasslands. "Just can't see Bone letting any creek get the best of him...Didn't ya'll say he was in some kind of special combat outfit in the Marine Corps?"

Loraine nodded. "What they call Recon Marines...They went behind the lines of the enemy, sometimes swimming from their boats out in the ocean to the shore at night...a lot of it underwater."

Fiona nodded. "See?"

Loraine gazed skyward then back to Fiona. "Hope you're right."

Bone got to his feet, stepped over, and felt of his saddle blanket. "Well, that's fair to middlin' dry."

He looked at Bear Dog, then over at Hildebrandt. "Maybe we oughta saddle up an' see if we can locate a farmhouse or country store...Find out where the heck we are...Maybe use their phone an' call the captain."

Bear Dog cocked his head again at Bone.

He gave a short whistle at Hildebrandt. The big horse replied with a chuckle, grabbed one more bite of grass, and walked over to him.

Bone flipped the folded blanket over his back, pulled it up to his withers, and slid it back a little to smooth the hair.

Then he picked the saddle off the limb. "Leather's still a tad damp, but take a couple days to totally dry...it'll do. Ain't gonna spend a lotta time ridin' 'round sight-seein'."

Bone put the off-stirrup in the seat and slung his custom-made saddle onto the blanket. He pulled a bubble in the blanket up into the gullet, pushed the stirrup off the seat, where it fell to the right side, and then reached under Hildebrandt's belly to grab the cinch.

Bone fed the latigo through the cinch ring, threaded it through the front rigging D twice, sucked the saddle down, and tied it off with a half-hitch.

"That should do it, Amigo...Didn't pull it too tight, you're probably still a mite sore." He patted the side of Hildebrandt's neck.

Bone stuck his foot in the stirrup and swung into the saddle. He pointed east.

"Eastward ho, me hardies."

Hildebrandt broke into an easy single-foot toward the east. Bear Dog trotted along out in front.

Bone, Hildebrandt, and Bear Dog had traveled less than a quarter of a mile when they came to some old ruins in the scattered hardwood trees.

HILDEBRANDT & BEAR DOG

Bone sat his saddle and scanned the area a moment—taking in the collapsed, rotting logs, a large caved-in area with more logs, and an old well nearby lined with native stone.

"Now, what in the Sam Hill, guys? Looks for all the world like an old fort...or somethin' like it." He shook his head. "Sure don't recall any forts up this way."

Bone dismounted, ground-tied Hildebrandt, while Bear Dog sniffed around. He stepped over to the depression and pulled an old, weathered, and mostly rotted-away plank.

Bone studied it a moment as the wolf-dog padded over to see what he had picked up. "Looks like letterin', Pard...See a 'RT', maybe 'FORT'. Another 'F'...an 'I', then a, 'Z'? Huh?...A 'H', finally a 'GH'." He shook his head. "No idea...Oh, wait!."

Bone looked down at Bear Dog. "I'm a monkey's uncle, but looks like 'Fort Fitzhugh'...That makes no sense. There was a Fort Fitzhugh set up by volunteers of the Texas Rangers in 1847 in Cooke

County, headed by a Captain William Fitzhugh...But it was closed down an' abandoned in 1850...Was originally going to be the county seat, till they built Gainesville."

Bear Dog cocked his head again in an effort to understand Bone.

"There shouldn't be anything at all left here...nothin', *nada*, zip, *net, nein*."

Bear Dog growled and turned toward an old dirt road.

Three riders sat their horses at the edge of the clearing looking at Bone. One of them popped his battered hat to the back of his head.

"What ya got there, big man?"

Bone instantly got a bad vibe from the tone of the man's voice, dropped the piece of plank, and surreptitiously undid the snap holding his 500 in the holster. The hair along the back of Bear Dog stood up.

"You fellas takin' a survey, are you?"

The three laughed and exchanged glances.

The one on the far side looked at the first man. "He's kinda funny, ain't he, Rufus?"

"Tryin' to be, 'peers like, Alwin."

"Yeah, mebe oughta be in Vaudeville...or the Chautauqua Circuit."

They laughed again.

The third man pointed to Hildebrandt. "Hey, looky, Ruf, that's some kinda good-lookin' horse back 'ar...'bout a big sombitch."

"Do believe yer right, Lank...do believe."

Rufus straightened up in his saddle. "Might look purty good sittin' on him, 'stead of this nag."

Bone grinned and looked back at Hildebrandt, then back at the tobyman. "You might look pretty good dead, too, Slick."

Rufus raised his hands. "Whoa, looky there, ya'll, he done got me plumb scared...Meby oughta kill that ugly mutt first..." He looked at Lank and Alwin. "What do ya'll think?"

Bone shook his head. "Ooo, big mistake, there, Rufus. He doesn't take kindly to being called 'ugly'...much less a 'mutt'...do you, Big Guy?"

Bear Dog's lips curled up from his usual smile to a vicious-looking snarl, showing his full inch-long white fangs as a deep growl rumbled from his chest.

"Oh, boy." Bone nodded. "Yeah, now he's pissed."

Lank, the nearest to Bear Dog, was the first to draw his Colt. Rufus, and Alwin followed suit.

Bone glanced at Bear Dog and grimaced. "Now, they've gone an' done it, haven't they?" His hand moved like a striking cottonmouth as the .50 caliber handgun cleared the leather...

Loraine, Fiona, and Mason trotted along the bank of the Elm Fork carefully scanning both sides of the creek.

"Water's already goin' down." Mason held his field glasses to his eyes and panned along the far bank.

Loraine nodded. "Quite a bit since just this morning...Could I borrow those glasses, Mason?"

"Sure." He lifted the strap from around his neck and handed the military-style glasses he had from his days in the cavalry over to Loraine. She was sitting next to him on the bay horse he had gotten from the corral for her.

She panned down to the south, then looked back up. "There's a bend down there about a hundred and fifty yards that's a bit wider than above and below it...Would have been a good place for Hildebrandt to have made it out to that side."

Fiona reached for the glasses and Loraine handed them to her. She studied the bend Loraine pointed out, then took them down.

"Would say you're right, Loraine...The way the creek is dropping...There's a bridge...or at least there was...down at the road that leads over to Mountain Springs from Valley View...We could cross there."

Mason glanced at her. "How far, Hon?"

She shook her head. "No more'n a mile, I would guess."

Loraine didn't wait, but turned her mount to the right and nudged the gelding into a lope. Mason and Fiona were quick to follow.

They had gone less than a hundred yards when a gunshot echoed across the hills and scattered trees from the east. It was followed instantly by several other smaller caliber shots, then a second louder one.

Loraine instantly reined to a full stop and looked across the creek to the other side, then at Fiona and Mason.

"That was Bone's .50 cal...Heard it enough to know it anywhere..."

She kicked the horse into a full gallop.

§§§

CHAPTER FOUR

COOKE COUNTY

A loud roar startled the horses. It wasn't from one of the guns—it was from Bear Dog as the black fury launched his body through the air at Link.

The two-hundred pound engine of destruction hit the one-hundred and sixty pound highwayman. The momentum carried them from the man's saddle into Alwin and his horse as the wolf-dog engulfed Lank's entire face in his monstrous maw.

The horse screamed in terror at the snarling, black menace next to him on the ground, mauling Link. He began crow-hopping as Alwin's pistol discharged in the air.

Bone fired a .50 caliber slug into the center of Rufus' chest, blowing him from the saddle—dead when he hit the ground behind his horse.

Rufus' dying nervous reaction caused him to fire his Colt a split-second after Bone's bullet hit him as he left the saddle. The shot missed Bone by inches and buried itself in the dirt to his left.

Simultaneously, Lank's screams of fear, already muffled by Bear Dog's mouth covering his face, were abruptly stopped by the crunching sound of the powerful jaws closing.

Alwin was thrown from his pitching horse to the ground. He scrambled quickly to his feet and snapped a quick shot from his Colt at Bone.

The man's hurried, panicky shot was off by a foot, but Bone's return fire was not.

A pink cloud erupted in the air as Alwin's head exploded like a ripe cantaloupe when the .400 grain lead slug hit him between the eyes.

The silence was deafening as Bone surveyed the carnage in front of him. The white cloud of gunsmoke from the .45s drifted off in the soft breeze.

"That's enough, Bear Dog."

The big animal walked away from Lank's body, blood still dripping from his muzzle, over to Bone.

The entire action was over in less than two seconds.

He looked down at Bear Dog. "Lord love a duck, Son, what the hell's goin' on?...Looks like a damn movie scene...But this is real."

Loraine, Fiona, and Mason galloped into the small farming community of Mountain Springs and headed toward the bridge.

The wooden and steel structure was still standing. There were several men close by apparently trying to inspect it for damage from the surging water.

Loraine slid her horse to a stop. She looked at the men.

"Still standin', I see."

"Yessum, but ain't safe, not by a long shot...Gonna have to shore up the supports when the water goes down some more."

Loraine nodded. "Close enough." She kicked her horse in the ribs with her moccasined heels. "Hyaaah." The long split reins were a perfect length to sling from side-to-side as she headed the animal across the one-hundred foot long bridge.

The men all shouted.

"Hey! Hey, lady! You cain't cross. Just said ain't safe!"

Fiona bumped Spot into a gallop and headed after Loraine. "Too late to argue, Mister. She's made up her mind. Where she goes...we go."

Mason just shrugged his shoulders at the men and kicked his roan gelding, Red, into a gallop behind Loraine and Fiona.

The three horses thundered across the wooden planks of the bridge which were only inches above the water of the still flooded creek.

The men watched with grimaced, scrunched-up faces, fully expecting the bridge to collapse any second, sending the three into the muddy water—it didn't.

The first man turned to the others. "Well, fellers, reckon she's stronger'n we thought."

Flynn's horse just cleared the opposite end when the bridge groaned, sagged, and the far end fell into the churning water.

The three men exchanged glances.

Loraine headed her gelding back upstream on an old dirt road in the direction of the shots they'd heard.

She looked over her shoulder at Fiona. "How far back do you think that gunfire was?"

"Maybe a mile...possibly two."

Mason caught up with them. "We best slack off a bit. These guys can't keep this pace up."

Loraine nodded and eased back on her reins enough to slow to a trot. Fiona and Mason matched her speed.

They looked up as a wild-eyed horse galloped past them, kicking and bucking.

Loraine watched the terrified animal run by. "Believe we're headed the right way."

Mason nodded. "Would say let's just follow his tracks back down the road, bound to lead somewhere."

HILDEBRANDT & BEAR DOG

Bone pulled two replacement rounds from his belt and replaced the empties in his 500. He picked up the brass and slipped them in his pocket out of habit.

"Well, need to figure out how far to town it is...Shouldn't be over ten or twelve miles. 'Course ya'll understand that's a swag, now."

Hildebrandt looked up at him, a clump of grass hung from his mouth, but not for long. It soon disappeared inside to be chewed up. He went back down for another bite.

Bear Dog sat down and looked up at Bone, his head cocked to the right.

"Ha, you look like the RCA dog in the picture listening to that Gramophone thing." He chuckled. "Wish you could talk."

Bear Dog snapped his head to the left at the dirt road. Bone followed his gaze, and then heard the sound of three horses trotting along the packed dirt.

In a moment, the three riders appeared from behind the trees around a bend.

"Bone!" Loraine kicked her horse back into a gallop toward Bone and Bear Dog.

Hildebrandt looked up again, then went back down to continue grazing.

Loraine reined the horse hard, bailed from the saddle before he was completely stopped like a calf-roper, and sprinted over to the big man. She jumped in the air, throwing her arms around his neck, wrapping her legs about his hips, and covered his face with kisses.

"You're safe! You're safe!"

"Whoa, Pard. Hang on." He lifted her easily off his hips and set her on the ground in front of him. "Where did all that lovey-dovey stuff come from?"

Loraine's face took on a shocked look. "What?"

Bone looked up as Fiona and Mason rode up and dismounted. "Who're your friends?"

"Huh?"

"An' what'n hell's goin' on? Last thing I recall before we crawled out of that creek was I was takin' you fishin' at Possum Kingdom Lake." He shook his head. "Ain't a lake within miles of here, far as I can tell...What's the deal?"

Loraine touched a bruise on his temple."

"Ow, that smarts."

She looked at Fiona and Mason. "Oh, my God...He's got partial amnesia."

Bone looked down at her. "I got what, Pard?"

She took his arm. "Let's go sit down over there under that big oak, Bone...As you would say, 'Grab your butt, Pard, you ain't gonna believe this'."

"Are you crazy?...Always knew I was three gallons of crazy in a two gallon bucket...but have I rubbed off on you since we became partners?"

Loraine smiled. "You may think so when we finish."

They headed over to the big shade tree. Mason loosened the horses girths a bit and picketed them on the grass near Hildebrandt before joining the others.

A full hour later, Bone stood, walked in a tight circle three times, and sat back down.

"We got what?"

"We were married three years ago, in Faye's back yard...Are you sorry?"

"Sorry? Stars an' candy bars, Baby...No!." Bone chuckled. "I fell in love with you on first sight..."

"Then why did you give me such a hard time for five years?"

Bone shrugged. "I was scared to death you wouldn't like me...so the wall went up...an' if you'd wore pigtails, I would have dunked 'em in the ink well...Guess you eventually saw through all that."

"You think?...You told me about the girl you fell in love with in college. The head twirler, an' she dumped you." Loraine got to her feet, hugged him and kissed him hard.

"All right, ya'll, enough kissie-face."

They glanced over at Fiona and grinned.

Bone looked back at Loraine, then Fiona and Mason, and shook his head. "I didn't know I didn't know, but you told me I didn't know. Now, I know I didn't know...but I now I know."

Mason frowned and looked at Loraine. "What's he sayin'?"

Loraine shook her head. "That's just Bone being Bone...That part's still there."

He turned to Fiona and Mason. "An' Fiona an' Mason are for sure an' by golly my great-grandparents?"

"Uh-huh."

"Slap Aunt Gussie in the face." He shook his head. "So I guess there's no sense in contactin' Sheriff Compton 'bout all our dead friends over there?"

"Not hardly. He won't be elected for a hundred years...Not even born yet."

"Ouch, Babe, you're givin' me a headache." He looked at her. "Guess that proves Gibbs rule eight...'Never take anything for granted'."

Mason turned to Loraine. "Who's Gibbs?"

She rolled her eyes. "Later, Mason."

§§§

CHAPTER FIVE

COOKE COUNTY

"And we've been here three years?"

Loraine smiled. "Four."

"Boy, don't that blow your dress up?" He looked at her. "We've been *married* for three years?"

"Right."

"We sleep together an' play grab-ass?"

"Well...Yeah."

Bone stood up, shook his head and kicked the dirt with the toe of his Apache-style moccasin. "Dang!"

"What?"

He frowned. "Had the hots for you for five years before we came here an' you say we been foolin' around for the last three...an' I don't remember a minute of it...If that don't hair-lip the Pope."

"We'll catch up later."

His head snapped to her. "How much later?"

Loraine backhanded him across the chest. "Damn you, Bone...I've been worrying myself sick and you want to have sex."

He shrugged. "Well?"

She exhaled. "Do you remember *Anompoli Lawa*, the Chickasaw Shaman?...His white name is Winchester Ashalatubbi, he's a medical doctor."

Bone shook his head. "No clue."

"We met him early on." Loraine looked at Fiona. "Maybe we can send him a telegram when we get to Gainesville...see if he can come down from Ardmore and help you fill in the gap in your memory any." She glanced over at the three bodies. "After we go by Sheriff Walt Durbin's office an' let him know about you an' Bear Dog's handy-work."

Mason grimaced. "Oh, reminds me...Forgot. What with lookin' for Bone an' all."

"Forgot what?"

He reached in his pocket, pulled out a yellow flimsey and handed it to Loraine. "Meant to give this to you. Came right after ya'll left this mornin'."

Bone looked over her shoulder as she opened it, then up at Mason. "From a Deputy Sheriff Platt in Jacksboro?"

He and Loraine read the telegram and exchanged glances.

Bone raised his eyebrows. "Looks like things ain't a whole lot different than back home...Guess we get to put on our cop shoes, Pard."

"We've never taken them off, you big galoot. It would take eight or nine of the kind of books that novelist Ken Farmer writes to tell all the stuff we've been into since we got here...We just finished a case where we had to track down Butch Cassidy an' the Sundance Kid in the Wichita Mountains up in the Oklahoma Territory."

"Get outta town...Butch an' Sundance?"

"They helped us take care of an outlaw gang an' we joined up to find some Spanish gold."

"So we're rich?"

Loraine shook her head. "We let them keep it after they gave back the two Army payrolls they stole in a couple of train robberies...They headed to Fort Worth last week to cash in a bunch of gold doubloons and have a good time."

"Kiss a fat baby." Bone shook his head, then banged the side of it with his hand.

Fiona stared at him. "What are you doin'?"

"Trying to knock some memories back. Remember everything from our time...but nothin' here from before me an' the boys crawled out of the flood...Got thumped in the head by a big limb."

Loraine frowned. "Don't think that'll do it, Bone...Your head's too thick for your hands. Why I want to contact *Anompoli Lawa*. He says, 'If you go to the past, then you are part of the past...and always have been."

"Huh...Kinda goes along with Einstein's theory of Special Relativity...'The past, present, an' future all exist at the same time'."

Mason rubbed his temples. "Now you're makin' my head hurt."

"Hey, we can also get hold of Lucy..."

"Lucy's still here?"

Loraine raised her shapely eyebrows. "Yes, Bone...Remember, she doesn't get rescued until 2014."

"Oh, duh, right."

"We helped her after her spacecraft crashed near Aurora in 1897, four years ago...Mason's sister and brother-in-law, Cletus and Mary Lou Wilson, are the ones that took her in when Mason an' Bodie found her."

"Bodie?"

"Bodie Hickman, Texas Ranger."

"Oh, hey, heard of him in our time. Pretty famous Ranger."

"That too, but Lucy saved your life here...Actually brought you back. You died."

"I what?"

"You jumped in front of a bad guy fixing to shoot Fiona an' took the bullet...Probably why we came here to begin with...if you believe in that sort of thing."

"How's that?"

Loraine looked at Fiona. "If Bone hadn't taken the bullet...he never would have existed because you would have been killed."

Bone nodded. "Another of Einstein's theories..."

"What's that?"

"What he called the 'grandfather paradox'. If someone goes back in time and kills their own grandfather they would cease to exist...or grandmother."

"But it wasn't you, Bone."

"I know, gra..."

She wagged her finger at him. "Ah-uh, great grandson or not...don't go there, Bone. Call me Fiona or I'll kill you myself."

"Oh, okay...Well, anyway, that's what he said."

Loraine nodded. "We saw that grandfather paradox thing actually happen."

"We did?"

"Tell you about that later...We'd better head out, be dark-thirty time we get to

Gainesville, then to Faye's...That's where we've lived, pretty much, since we got here...along with Padrino."

"Padrino's here, too?"

"Yeah, he can tell you about that when we get there."

"Wow, okie-dokie." He looked at Loraine again with a twinkle in his eye. "An' we're married, huh?"

"Bone, I'm going to hurt you."

He cocked his head like Bear Dog and squinted his eyes. "Somethin' tells me that you can, too. What else don't I remember?"

"Well, in Jacksboro, out at Sewell Park, you wanted me to show you some of my Kung Fu techniques...and you would try to stop me." She laughed. "Didn't work. I put you on the ground about three times, then threw you close to eight feet over my head...an' that's when you told me you loved me."

"That really happened?"

"We were there, Bone. Saw it all...along with Lucy, Doctor Ashlatubbi an' Bodie."

He looked over at Fiona, then at Mason. "Makes sense. Never had been whipped before." He shook his head. "Butter my butt an' call me a biscuit...eight feet, huh?"

"Pretty close."

Bone chuckled and his eyes widened as he turned to Loraine. "*My Heart is an Open Book*...Did I sing that to you?"

"You did...Must be gettin' some of your memories back."

"Ooolale."

Mason shook his head. "Ya'll talk so odd."

Bone and Mason unsaddled the road agent's horses.

"They probably won't go far, there's plenty of grass."

Loraine glanced at Mason. "Except for the one that ran past us down the road, buckin' an' fartin'...He was walleyed crazy."

"Somebody'll catch him when he calms down."

"That was Bear Dog's doin's. Big fella was right beside him removin' Lank's face. The one called Alwin was in the saddle,...Would scare me, too. He bucked good old Alwin off an' cut a chogi for parts unknown."

Bear Dog looked up at Bone and whined. "Yeah, you, Fuzz-bucket...Don't try to deny it."

He laid down and covered his muzzle with his paws.

"But, I'm glad you did, gave me time to take care of the leader, Rufus."

Bear Dog got to his feet and stuck his paw out. Bone shook it. "Good job, Son."

Loraine smiled. "He is kinda handy to have around...Aren't you, Boy?"

Bear Dog chuffed as Hildebrandt nickered.

Bone looked at the big horse walking up. "They saved my bacon, more ways than one today." He snugged Hildebrandt's cinch, stuck his foot in the stirrup and swung aboard.

Fiona glanced at them. "Bone's the only person I know that doesn't have to hop to mount a horse that big. I almost have to for Spot." She forked him.

"How long you been ridin' a mule?"

"Oh, about four years, Bone. Renegade Apache shot my horse, Diablo, out from under me up the in the Wichitas...Love this guy, he's smooth as silk."

Loraine mounted her gelding and they headed north toward Gainesville. She and Bone rode side-by-side.

"What road is this, Pard? Don't recognize a thing."

"Burns City Road.

"You're blowin' smoke."

"Kid you not."

"Be darned...Do miss my Thing."

Mason's head snapped over at Bone. "Your what?"

Loraine giggled. "It's uh...a motor car."

"Humpf...Seen some of those. Noisy an' smelly..." He shook his head and frowned. "Never catch on."

Bone and Loraine exchanged glances.

§§§

CHAPTER SIX

GAINESVILLE, TEXAS

The sun neared the western horizon creating silver linings on the low scattered stratus clouds as the four rode into Gainesville. They turned to the west off Grand Avenue onto Main Street and trotted their horses across the Pecan

Creek bridge to the red brick, two-story Cooke County jail.

They dismounted and tied up to the rings on the iron posts out front. Mason opened the door, stood back and let Fiona and Loraine enter first, then he nodded at Bone. Bear Dog went in on Bone's heels.

Former Texas Ranger, now Sheriff Walt Durbin of Cooke County, looked up through the open door from his office to the deputy area and saw them come in.

"Hey, ya'll come on in." He got to his feet and walked around his desk to greet the four as they entered the deputy area.

"Are ya'll lost or did you finally decide to come into town and pay a long overdue visit?"

Mason shook Walt's hand. "In a roundabout way."

"In a roundabout way what?"

While he was waiting on Mason's excuse, he shook a bewildered Bone's hand, then gave Fiona and Loraine each a hug.

"If you're wonderin' why Bone's expression is like a goose that just woke up...he kinda did."

"What're you talkin' 'bout, Mason?"

"He has no idea who you are...Well, he knows who you are, but doesn't know you."

"Think I need to sit down. You're not makin' a whole lot of sense...Ya'll come in the office."

They all went in and sat down.

Mason turned his chair backward, straddled the seat, and propped his arms on the slat-back. "To make a long story long, Walt..."

Thirty minutes later, Mason and Loraine finished bringing Walt up to date.

"...So, you probably need to send a couple deputies out to old Fort Fitzhugh with a wagon an' pick the bodies up before they start drawin' buzzards...if they haven't already."

Walt leaned back in his sheriff-style swivel chair, looked at Mason, then at Bone, grinned, and shook his head. "Swear to God, Big Man, you can stir up more crap than the ground's keeper at the Fort Worth Livestock Show an' Rodeo."

"So I've heard...Walt, is it?"

The sheriff raised his eyebrows and stared at Bone for a minute. "An' you have no recollection of meetin' me?"

Bone shook his head and shrugged.

Walt looked toward the door. "Bertram...you and Marquis get in here."

The two middle-aged deputies bumped into each other tryin' to enter the door at the same time.

"One at the time, boys, one at the time."

Bertram entered followed by Marquis. "Yessir?"

"Ya'll get the wagon an' go out to old Fort Fitzhugh. Got three bodies that Bone and Bear Dog here sent to claim their reward or punishment from their maker this afternoon. Bring 'em into Doc Wellman. He'll know what to do."

Bertram frowned. "Reward or punishment?...Don't folla, Sheriff."

He pointed out the door. "Just go!...An' don't hurt anybody on the way."

"Sir?"

"Out! Out!"

The two deputies scrambled back through the door, bumping each other again.

Walt shook his head and rolled his eyes after they left. "Lead me to an early grave."

Bone nodded. "Yeah, got a few like them at the police department back where we...or when we...uh, come..."

"Know all about it, Bone. You, Loraine, an' Padrino have been here for four years."

"Oh, right." He looked at Loraine. "How come it is everybody knows everything, but me?"

"Because you got your head thumped an' nearly drowned, you big oaf."

"Oh, yeah...I did remember the song, though. That's a start ain't it?"

"Yes, it is."

"An' you don't remember ya'll an' Bass Reeves, takin' down that gang out to kidnap Teddy Roosevelt in the Kiamichi Wilderness back when he was Assistant Secretary of the Navy?"

"Wow! No, but sure would like to...Bass Reeves an' Teddy Roosevelt? Dang straight."

Loraine looked at him. "Brushy Bill Roberts was there, too."

"Brushy Bill? I'dn't he the guy that said he was really Billy the Kid?"

Fiona turned to Bone. "He was Billy the Kid. He an' his friend, Sheriff Pat Garrett faked his death in '81. He took off for Mexico for a couple of years, then came back as Brushy Bill Roberts...Became a livestock detective for the railroad..."

Bone smiled and nodded. "He had experience there."

"Right...Bill then was a Pinkerton Detective, and then a Special Deputy US Marshal like me. He went with Teddy down to Cuba as a member of the Rough Riders in the war against Spain."

"Well, guess he survived, 'cause he died of a heart attack in 1950, think it was, in Hico, Texas...Quite a life." He looked at Loraine, Fiona, and Mason. "An' we all worked with Bass protectin' Teddy Roosevelt?"

"We did."

"Shoot fire...Have got to catch up on all that stuff. Feel like I'm missin' out...Bass Reeves, Billy the Kid, an' Teddy...wow, who knew?"

"As well as Ranger Bodie Hickman...That's the general idea, Bone." Loraine whacked him on the shoulder.

Walt turned to Mason. "Guess you heard about the Jack County sheriff goin' missin'?"

Mason nodded. "Yeah, got a telegram 'bout it. Was going to send Bone an' Loraine over to Jacksboro to see what they could find out...They have better detective skills than I do."

"If you just got a telegram, chances are you didn't get the whole of it."

"Meanin'?"

"Jip Coltrane's wife committed suicide. Hung herself in the barn...an' his sixteen-year old daughter, Alice, also disappeared the next day."

"Jip?"

"Real name's James but been called Jip most of his life."

Bone glanced at Loraine, then back to Walt. "They think Coltrane might have just run off?"

Walt shook his head. "Not likely...Didn't pack nothing an' none of his horses were gone...He just vanished."

He opened a drawer and took out a manilla envelope. "The local coroner took some Strand-type pictures of the wife's body, before and after they cut her down."

He handed the envelope to Bone.

Loraine glanced at it while Bone opened the top. "What's Strand-style photography?"

"A new type of photography developed by a guy named Strand. Looks more true-to-life than the old stuff that looked lots like a paintin'."

She nodded. "That's good for cop work."

Loraine stood next to Bone as he spread the photographs out on Walt's desk for them to study.

They carefully looked them over, then glanced at each other.

"What do you see, Pard?"

"Something's not right, Bone."

"Uh-huh."

Mason, Fiona, and Walt crowded closer so they could see the pictures.

Fiona looked at Bone. "What is it?"

He turned to Walt. "They said she hung herself in the barn...right?"

"Right."

Bone pointed at the picture of a thirty-five to forty-year old woman hanging by a hemp rope from a rafter in a barn.

"What's missin'?"

"Huh?"

"What's missin'?"

Fiona looked up at Bone. "Ah...What did she stand on?"

"Exactly...Her feet are almost two feet from the ground...no stool or anything else in the area. How did she do that?"

Loraine studied the close-ups of the body at the coroner's office. She leaned over, then looked up at Walt.

"Do you have a magnifying glass?"

"Do." He opened a desk drawer and took a four-inch diameter magnifying glass with a four-inch handle out and handed it to Loraine.

She nudged Bone and held the glass over the woman's neck.

Walt handed a written report of the body to Bone. He scanned it and pointed to an area on the body.

Loraine looked, and then nodded.

"What is it?" Flynn's face showed he was getting perturbed.

Bone looked up. "One, her hyoid bone is crushed."

Walt frowned. "So? She hung herself."

"She was hung all right, but..."

"What do you mean, 'but'?"

He turned to Fiona. "When a person commits suicide by hanging themselves, as we mentioned, nothin' to stand on...that's a problem. Plus the rope is always skewed a little to the side, creating abrasions an' bruises...the hyoid bone is never damaged."

Flynn shook his head. "Not followin'."

Loraine pointed to the picture and held the glass over her neck. "No abrasions or bruises, and the hyoid is crushed."

Bone shrugged. "As Sherlock Holmes would say, 'The game is afoot'..." His gaze scanned everyone's face. "She was murdered...strangled, to be exact."

§§§

CHAPTER SEVEN

SHERIFF'S OFFICE

"You think Coltrane did it?"

Bone raised a single eyebrow at Walt. "I think that's what someone wants us to believe."

"Why do you say that?"

HILDEBRANDT & BEAR DOG

The big man looked at Loraine, then back to Walt. "It's too pat...Somebody went to a lot of trouble to stage this. If it were a crime of passion...which is far and away the biggest cause of domestic violence in the country...Coltrane wouldn't have gone to all this trouble...There's something else."

Flynn looked at Sheriff Durbin. "See, Walt, told you he was a better detective than me."

"By the way, Sheriff, how did you get all that information that's not in this report?" Bone held it up.

Walt pointed over to a small black box with a crank handle on the side mounted on the wall. "Called a tele-phone."

Mason nodded. "We just got one in the Sheriff's office in Jacksboro right before I retired...They are handy, alright."

Bone and Loraine pulled out their Galaxy 7 phones and held them up.

She grinned. "About ninety-five percent or more of the people in our time carry their own personal phone...They're wireless."

"Plus, they also take pictures." Bone set his on camera and showed Walt the image on the screen. "Instantly."

"We can contact anyone who has one almost anywhere in the world...in minutes."

Walt looked at Loraine. "You're funnin' me...Sounds like magic."

She and Bone shook their heads.

Bone shrugged. "A lot of new technology is confused for 'magic', Walt...Can't do anything with 'em here, though, except take pictures...Have to have a big tower to send any messages wirelessly...an' they don't exist yet and won't for almost another eighty years...Plus, would have to have some other of these to send 'em to."

Loraine took Walt's picture, turned her phone around and went to her gallery. She opened his photo and used her fingers to enlarged it to an extreme close-up.

Walt rocked back in his chair. "My God...that's amazin'. You can even see individual hairs in my mustache." He shook his head. "Son-of-a-gun."

Loraine smiled. "Can come in real handy in crime work." She frowned. "Just have to be prudent with the usage 'cause this thing uses electricity an' we have to rig up a way to recharge the battery when we use it up."

"We do?"

"Yes, Bone. Show you later."

"Was wonderin' 'bout that...Oh, uh, is that before or after we catch up..."

"Bone?...Gonna hurt you."

He giggled.

She looked at the others. "One thing about it, he may have lost part of his memory, but his personality is intact."

"Carved in stone, Babe, carved in stone...Been me for a long time. Don't know how to be anybody else."

Loraine rolled her eyes. "I know."

Fiona and Mason laughed—they'd been around Bone for almost the full four years he and Loraine had been in this time frame.

Bone looked at Mason. "How long have you known Jip Coltrane?"

"Most of my life. We pretty much grew up together...school an' all. Even in the cavalry together." Mason paused and shook his head. "No way, no way in hell Jip could do this."

Loraine nodded. "That's the other reason you want us on this...the emotional involvement. Ya'll're friends."

"Pretty much...I can give you a lot of insight, but should probably stay out of it."

Bone smiled. "The way we work, too...Like Gibbs rule number ten, 'Never get personally involved on a case."

Mason frowned. "That's twice you've mentioned this Gibbs guy."

78

Loraine turned to him. "He's a uh...kind of cop from our time."

"Must be a good one,"

Bone nodded. "Is, plus, he's a Marine...Where do you think Coltrane went an' how?"

Mason took a breath. "Well, that's the other thing...Think he knows who's behind all this an' he went after 'em."

Loraine glanced at Bone. "That what your gut is sayin'?"

"Yup, exactly...Always trust your gut...then figure out why it's tellin' you what it is."

"To answer your question, my gut says he thinks whoever he's after headed to the Kiamichis an' the Seven Devil Hills...which ya'll know pretty well."

"So I'm told...What makes you think it's there, Mason?"

"Deputy Marvin Platt in Jacksboro that sent the telegram, also worked for me...He found a wadded up piece of paper in the barn near the body..."

"Yeah, saw the reference at the bottom of the flimsey...said Seven Devil Hills, didn't it?"

"Did, Bone." He turned to Walt. "See."

'Yeah."

Loraine looked at Flynn. "What do you think the deal with the daughter, Alice, is?"

Mason frowned. "That's got me stumped."

"We'll find out, Pard."

She turned to Bone. "See any sense in lookin' over the crime scene?"

He shook his head. "Naw, Babe. Bag of bear claws they've stomped all over...Be contaminated as hell...Waste of time."

She nodded. "Figured."

He looked at Walt again. "Another question...How did he leave?...If he didn't take any of his horses."

"I may know the answer, Bone."

They looked at Mason.

"Only thing I can figure is, know he's got relatives just outside Clarksville with a big ranch in the Red River bottom...Guessin' he rode the train there an' picked up a horse or two from his kin...Their place is 'bout thirty-mile south of the Kiamichis, on this side of the Red."

Bone pursed his lips. "Easy enough to find out if he rode the train from the conductor. Santa Fe train that runs that east-west route will probably use the same crew...comin' an' goin'. Most railroads do."

"Think we need a picture of him or anything, Bone?"

He looked at Mason. "Wouldn't hurt...If one's available."

"Not that I have, Bone. I'll write out a good description of him for ya'll, though."

"That'll help." He glanced at Loraine. "Think of anything else, Pard?"

"Just this." She looked at Mason. "Any reason *why* come to mind?...Motive, in other words."

"Not really, Loraine...The Coltrane family has a bushel basket of money though...land, cattle, silver mine in Arizona..."

"Always look for the money, Pard. Always look for the money."

She shook her head in exasperation. "Times don't seem to change that much, do they?"

"Neither do people...an' they control the times."

The phone on the wall jangled twice. Walt got up, walked over to it, picked the receiver up from the hook on the left side and gave the crank on the right four quick turns.

"Sheriff Durbin...Uh-huh. Don't say?" He glanced at Bone and them. "Keep an eye out for 'em. Thanks for the information." He hung the receiver back on the hooks.

Walt looked at the group. "That was the constable down at Mountain Springs...said three crazy people, two women an' a man rode across the bridge down there seconds before it collapsed into the creek."

Bone glanced at Loraine, Fiona, and Mason with a grin. "Wonder who that could have been?"

FAYE SKEAN'S BOARDING HOUSE

Bone, Loraine, Fiona, and Mason tied up out front of a stately Queen Ann three-story red brick house. Faye had turned her home into a boarding house after her husband was killed in the War of Northern Aggression.

Loraine glanced at the others. "We'll put the horses and Fiona's mule in the carriage house an' grain 'em after we go in an' bring everyone up to date.

Bone looked around. "There's a carriage house?"

She nodded. "Yes, Bone, it's out back."

"Huh?...Handy."

"If we don't have to go anywhere for a while, we take them out to Walt an' Frances Ann's horse ranch outside of town...Lot more room. They can run in a big pasture."

"Makes sense."

They stepped up on the porch and Mason opened the ornate half-glass front door for the others an' Bear Dog.

The four stepped in the foyer where Mason hung his Stetson on the brass hooks on each side of the mirror above the entry table.

Padrino could see them from his chair in the parlor through the open double pocket doors.

"Hey, ya'll are back...an' brought the Flynns with you."

They stepped on in. Most of the other residents of the boarding house were seated around the large parlor either reading or talking.

HILDEBRANDT & BEAR DOG

Bear Dog went directly to his spot in front of the fireplace and promptly laid down.

In addition to Padrino, there was Silke and Haven Justice, look-alike cousins, both Pinkerton Detectives. The only obvious difference in the two was Silke, the oldest, had long strawberry blonde hair, while Haven, two years younger, had long dark auburn hair with a few streaks of red.

Rawboned, redheaded, Texas Ranger Bodie Hickman sat in a chair across from Padrino. His wife, Annabel, from Alabama, was in the kitchen helping Faye prepare supper.

A long boarding house dining table was in the next room between the parlor and the kitchen. Meals were served three times a day at set times. Everyone ate together.

"Bone you look like you took a bath in your clothes."

"Did, Padrino...Me, Hildebrandt, an' Bear Dog fell in Elm Fork when the bank collapsed under us."

"Durin' the flood?"

Bone looked confused as the strawberry blonde asked the question.

Loraine leaned over to him. "That's Silke Justice...told you about her."

"Oh, right. Uh...Yeah, uh, Silke. Carried us 'bout ten miles downstream..."

"Do what?" She shot to her feet.

Faye and Annabel entered the room from the dining room where they were setting out plates when they heard the conversation.

Loraine stepped forward. "Guess I'd best go ahead an' explain..."

§§§

CHAPTER EIGHT

FAYE SKEAN'S BOARDING HOUSE

"Always figured your head was too hard an' thick for somethin' like this."

Loraine glanced over at Silke. "You'd think. But guess getting whacked along with almost drowning..."

"Three times." Bone held up three

fingers.

She turned to Bone. "You said you were only hit on the head with a big branch once."

"Yeah, Babe, but do kinda remember blackin' out three times when we got pulled under...That's all still fuzzy."

"Glad we had Walt call up to Ardmore an' have the sheriff get a message to *Anompoli Lawa*."

"What time's his train get here in the morning?"

Loraine turned to Padrino. "Scheduled to arrive at ten."

"I'll take the carriage an' pick him up."

Fiona grinned. "Bet he makes us build a sweatlodge."

Bone looked at her. "For what?"

"You."

"Oh, boy...Hope it's not like the one Padrino made me get in that time back in 2014."

"He'll have us build a Chickasaw sweatlodge...Loraine an' I will get inside with you an' thrash you all over with fresh-cut cedar branches...naked."

"Ya'll?"

Fiona shook her head. "You."

"Whoopee."

Silke giggled. "The best part is the dowsing with buckets of ice water right when you come out." She looked over at Haven. "That'll be our job, Cuz."

"Oh, wow, fun."

Bone looked at the pair. "Paybacks are hell."

Silke nodded. "An' talk is cheap."

Loraine got to her feet. "All right ya'll, enough. The idea is to help Bone get his memory back."

Bone shrugged. "I don't know, Babe, been doin' pretty good so far...except for not rememberin' us playin'..."

"Bone?" She raised one dark eyebrow and pointed a finger at him.

He chuckled. "Love gettin' your goat."

"You're going to think gettin' my goat when we reenact my Kung Fu demonstration."

Bone wiggled both eyebrows. "Can't wait."

GAINESVILLE DEPOT

Padrino waited on the platform between the red brick depot and the tracks of the southbound Gulf and Colorado Railroad.

The black, straight-stack, 4x4x2 locomotive bled off immense clouds of steam just past the platform, missing the people waiting either to get on or those getting off.

The engineer had stopped the train with the two passenger cars lined up at the platform for the travelers.

The third person to disembark down the steel steps of the first car was an elderly, white-haired Chickasaw. He was dressed in a black, three-piece suit, purple cravat, and a tall crown, uncreased, black felt Stetson, with a red-tailed hawk tail feather in the beaded hatband.

HILDEBRANDT & BEAR DOG

"Winchester!"

The Chickasaw Shaman turned to see a wiry, white-haired man near his own age waving at him. "Padrino!"

He walked rapidly toward the retired Marine, set his carpet bag and his black leather medical bag down, and the two friends embraced—pounding each other's back as men do.

"How was your trip?" Padrino stepped back and picked up the bags.

"No problems...You're looking well."

"Faye's been taking good care of me. Don't remember ever eating so much home cooking...except maybe when I was a kid visitin' my grandparents."

"Faye's a wonderful cook, all right."

"She saved you some venison sausage gravy, along with some of her hot buttermilk biscuits in the warmin' oven...We ate earlier, but she figured you'd be hungry when you got here."

He grinned as they walked toward the open-topped, black, Baroque carriage belonging to Faye out in front of the depot. "She figured correctly...Of course I can always eat Faye's venison sausage gravy an' biscuits."

Padrino nodded. "May have some more myself."

They both chuckled as they got in the carriage. Padrino put the bags behind the front seat, undid the reins from around the brake lever and double-clucked the matched, white stockinged sorrel geldings into a smooth single-foot.

"Now, what's this problem with Bone? The message from Walt was a bit cryptic."

"Well, not sure, except he seems to have partial amnesia."

"Partial amnesia?"

"Apparently...He, Hildebrandt, an' Bear Dog got swept away when the Elm Fork of the Trinity flooded. Bank gave way, dumpin' them in the flood...When they made it out 'bout ten miles downstream, he'd been whacked in the head at least once an' almost drowned three times."

"Knowing Bone, it's probably a good thing he got hit in the head...might have killed him otherwise."

"Marines die pretty hard."

"I can tell...Go on."

"He can remember everything prior to 2018, but from the time he an' Loraine came through that portal four years ago, up to the point of being in the creek yesterday...almost nothing."

"A four year gap?"

"Yep...He won't have any idea who you are except that we told him you were the Chickasaw Shaman, a licensed medical doctor, an' a doctor of divinity."

Anompoli Lawa nodded as he wiped the inside of his hat with a handkerchief, and then put it back on. "A start."

He looked over at Padrino as he pulled the team to a stop in front of Faye's. "Will most likely have to make him go through a sweatlodge treatment."

"What we figured...Got Silke an' Haven gatherin' the skins an' river rocks....I did it to him back in our time to make him more aware when he was first dealing with Lucy then...."

"Wouldn't hurt to have her here."

"Figured that, too...Bodie an' Flynn headed out at daylight to fetch her. Be back around noon or before, we figure."

"Good...Look forward to seeing the little lady."

"Yep, always a pleasure...Head on inside. I'll take the boys around to the carriage house an' stall 'em."

Winchester nodded, got out, grabbed his bags, and headed to the front porch.

Since it was a boarding house, he went on inside, knowing he was expected anyway. Plus, he'd been here many times in the last four years.

Winchester Ashalatubbi walked through the foyer after hanging his hat on the tree.

Fiona, Loraine, and Bone were waiting in the parlor.

"Winchester!" Fiona got to her feet, stepped over, and embraced the elderly Chickasaw.

Loraine followed right behind her and also hugged him.

Bone cocked his head as the Shaman turned to him. "*Chi-hòo-wah-bia-chi, chaffa ona.*" He bowed slightly in reverence. "How did you know the Chickasaw phrase for 'Go with God', my son?"

Bone rocked back on his heels. "Uh...I don't know, sir...It just came out. Wasn't sure what it meant until you just told me...Just knew it was the thing to say."

The Shaman glanced at the others. "I believe everything is there, it's just been tucked away in another corner."

"You're *Anompoli Lawa*, also known as Doctor Winchester Ashalatubbi?"

"That also come to you?"

Bone shook his head. "No, sir, Fiona an' Loraine told me."

"Good enough." He put his hand on Bone's shoulder. "I believe we can clear away the fog, Bone." His eyes twinkled.

"Sweatlodge?"

"You heard?"

He shrugged. "I was warned. My Padrino made me do one back in our time." Bone looked at Loraine. "Is it 'back' or 'forward', Babe?"

"No idea, Bone."

The Shaman smiled. "If you travel to the past, then you are part of the past...and always have been."

"They said you'd say that...When are we goin' to do that sweatlodge thing?"

"Sundown...You may have only water that I have blessed between now and then...no food."

"Uh-huh." He took a breath. "Joy."

Faye came in from the kitchen with Padrino who had entered through the back door after taking care of the horses at the carriage house.

"Winchester!" She gave him a big hug. "So good to see you. It's been too long."

"It has that, Faye...I understand you have something for me."

She glanced at Padrino. He shrugged.

"Come on into the kitchen. You can have your biscuits an' gravy at the breakfast table."

He looked at Bone. "Want to come in an' talk, Bone?"

"No...Not an' watch you eat. Figure the sweatlodge will be enough punishment for today."

Doctor Ashalatubbi chuckled as he followed Faye and Padrino back into the kitchen through the large dining room.

Bone turned to Fiona an' Loraine and opened his mouth, then his eyes widened and his head snapped in the direction of the front door.

"Lucy!"

The front door opened and a diminutive woman, a little less than five-feet tall, entered, followed by Bodie and Flynn.

"Oh, my...Bone, you're a mess."

He grinned. "Tell me something I don't know, *Annuna*." Bone gently hugged the small Annuniki alien.

Her spaceship had crashed at Aurora, Texas, northwest of Fort Worth, five years ago on April 17, 1897. The townspeople buried her mate and copilot in the local cemetery.

No one knew she survived until Flynn, Fiona, and Bodie found her in the nearby farm community of Paradise, Texas.

Flynn took her to his sister and brother-in-law's ranch in Cooke County. Cletus and Mary Lou Wilson took her in as an abandoned, mute child because she couldn't speak English at the time an' her size enabled her to pass as a juvenile."

"I could read you soon as we got into town...My goodness. It's good I came."

Bone nodded. "I felt you when ya'll were walking up the steps."

She nodded. "*Anompoli Lawa* and I should be able to help."

"You knew he was here?...Oh, silly question. Of course you did."

The pixie-haired woman smiled.

§§§

CHAPTER NINE

FAYE SKEAN'S BOARDING HOUSE

"When will the fire be ready, Silke?" Haven put another four-inch pecan log on the blaze.

Her cousin looked up from tying another willow branch to the center of the top of the dome-shaped sweatlodge.

"When there's an even bed of good coals about five inches thick."

"Be puttin' out a lots of heat."

"That's the point. Those granite river rocks we placed around the fire will be some kind of hot."

"That's when *Anompoli Lawa* will pour the blessed water on 'em, right?"

"After we set the finished lodge over it with the bed of coals in the center."

"Oh, I see."

"Hand me a couple of deerskins."

"Comin'."

Haven handed Silke the skins and helped her drape them on the willow frame, starting at the bottom. They tied each one to several of the willow support arches.

"Looks like it's goin' to take twelve or more skins,"

Silke nodded. "More like sixteen to get a good seal."

"You've done this before?"

"Well, haven't built one before, but saw the Chickasaw ladies build the one I had to get in for my Hatchet Woman Clan induction."

Hildebrandt watched the girls with his head stuck out the top of the half-door on the outside of his stall in the carriage house. He had been watching since they started and occasionally nodded and nickered.

Bear Dog lay at the bottom of the door of his friend's stall, also watching every move they made—his head would cock first to the right, then to the left as they worked.

Haven glanced over her shoulder at the pair. "They look like they know what we're doin'."

Silke grinned. "Probably know it's for Bone."

He stretched out on the longhorn skin rug in front of the big, brown, saddle-leather couch. Lucy laid beside him, holding his hand.

Anompoli Lawa sat in a nearby wing-back chair watching them with interest—even though he'd seen Lucy's healing energy work before. All the previous efforts were for serious physical wounds—this was all together something different.

"Goodness, Bone, parts of your mind are like scrambled eggs."

"Already knew that, Lucy."

"No, I mean different than normal."

Loraine, sitting on the couch beside them shook her head. "Ooo, that's scary."

"Bite me, Babe."

She leaned over his face. "You wish."

"Later."

"Close your eyes, Bone, and open to me."

"Right."

They both closed their eyes and a soft blue glow began to emanate from Lucy and slowly spread to engulf Bone in the aura.

Loraine leaned over to Fiona sitting beside her. "We better go get a large pitcher of fresh water. They'll both be asking for it when they come out of this."

Loraine and Fiona stepped around the pair and headed to the kitchen.

Padrino sat in a matching chair to the one Winchester was in. They exchanged glances and nodded, both knew what the tiny woman could do.

Loraine and Fiona came back in carrying a large ceramic pitcher, a quart Mason jar for Bone and a smaller glass for Lucy.

For some reason, the exchange of life energy from one person to another made both extremely dehydrated.

Lucy's little body quivered as tiny beads of sweat broke out on her forehead, causing her bangs to become damp.

Bone's breathing was deep and regular.

Faye watched the procedure with the others from a green velvet love seat next to *Anompoli Lawa's* chair. She turned to the Shaman.

"Maybe one day most of the human race will be able to do that."

He smiled. "Actually, dear lady, the laying on of hands for healing is mentioned throughout the Bible...from Acts to James, Matthew, and also First Timothy...It's been practiced for thousands of years."

"Why don't more people use it?"

"Because they get in the way."

Faye frowned, not totally understanding.

Finally, the glow subsided back into Lucy. She took a deep breath, opened her light brown eyes flecked with gold—they were the same as Bone and Padrino's. Lucy blinked rapidly several times, then looked up at Loraine and Fiona.

They helped her sit up and handed her a glass of water.

"Thank you."

Bone took another deep breath and blew it out, then he, too, sat up and reached for the full quart jar in Loraine's hand. He drained it without taking it from his lips.

"Wow."

Loraine looked at him. "Feel any better?"

He shook his head. "Some. I can see a lot of what went on since we got here, but it's like lookin' at it through a curtain."

The Shaman nodded. "The sweatlodge should clear much of that away. I'll go out and see how the ladies are progressing." He got to his feet.

Padrino got up and followed him. "Go with you."

They went out the back door and could see Silke and Haven working on tying the last of the skins on the top. Flynn and Bodie were helping and occasionally stirring the fire, arranging the coals so they heated the cantaloupe-sized rocks evenly.

Anompoli Lawa had grabbed his large medicine pouch before heading out to the backyard. He set it on a picnic table nearby, opened it, set several items on the table...his personal totem, a bear carved from a piece of lightning-riven oak, a small bag of sacred dogwood pollen, a four ounce brown jar of a liquid, and a bag of some of his Shamanistic powder he would use.

He looked to the west as the sun disappeared below the horizon, then to the east as the top edge of the full fall equinox moon appeared.

"The fire has stopped smokin', *Anompoli Lawa*."

"Thank you *Kowishto' Ihoo Hommá*, you may set the *wickiup* over the ring of coals after you place a couple of deer skins on each side for us to sit on."

"She nodded. "As you wish."

Haven leaned over to Silke. "What's that *Kowishto' Ihoo Hommá* mean?"

"It's my Chickasaw name, means Red Hair Woman."

"Oh, makes sense."

The Shaman turned to Padrino and reached inside his bag. "I'll go inside and change if you'll have Bone put this on and meet us back out here."

He handed him a folded piece of soft chamois, picked up the deerskin bag of powder, and headed to the back door.

Silke, Haven, Flynn, and Bodie picked up the dome-shaped *wickiup* and set it over the ring of rocks and glowing coals.

Flynn stood on his tiptoes trying to see over the lodge. "This is a lot taller than most *wickiups* I've seen."

Silke looked at him. "So Bone can stand up in there while Fiona and Loraine thrash him with those juniper branches we cut an' laid near the deerskins inside."

Bodie chuckled. "Wish we could watch that."

Silke grinned. "I expect we'll be able to hear him voice his discomfort out here."

"Yeah, but be a lot more fun to watch the big man squirm."

"I know."

They turned as they heard the back screen door slam to see *Anompoli Lawa* come down the stoop wearing only a soft breechclout of tanned doeskin chamois.

He also wore a beaded headdress and had a design painted on his face and chest in red ocher with black streaks. He carried an ornately decorated dried gourd in one hand.

The Shaman stepped to the table, picked up his bear totem, laid the gourd down, and opened the bag of sacred dogwood pollen.

He tossed a pinch to each of the four directions and one straight up in the air. Then he waved his totem over a bucket of water with a dipper inside chanting a blessing, sprinkling a powder in it, and nodded to Silke.

She took the bucket inside the *wickiup*, crawling through a four-foot high opening in the front with a deerskin hanging covering it. In a moment, she crawled back out.

Loraine and Fiona came out the back door, each was wearing only clean camisoles with their hair pulled back. The

Shaman had painted a Chickasaw design on their faces. They immediately entered the *wickiup*.

Anompoli Lawa blessed the buckets of water containing chunks of ice from the icebox in the house on either side of the opening with his bear totem and pinches of pollen. He turned and nodded toward the back door of the house.

Faye opened the door and led a blindfolded Bone down the steps, followed by Lucy. She had completely recovered and carried a terra-cotta bowl of brownish liquid. Bone, like the Shaman, wore only the breechclout.

Faye directed Bone to the opening. "Kneel down, Bone, and crawl inside."

He did as he was bid. Lucy followed him with the bowl and came right back out after giving it to *Anompoli Lawa*.

Inside, Fiona removed his blindfold. She and Loraine picked up the juniper branches and stood on either side of him.

"Cover yourself, Bone."

He glanced at Fiona, then Loraine as she pointed to his crotch.

"Ah, right."

They started swatting him all over his body with the prickly cedar branches.

"Ooo, ouch, aiiee, wow!...Smarts."

They hit him harder for talking.

"Take it, Bone."

He nodded at Fiona.

They thrashed him for a good five more minutes until the Shaman nodded. Fiona picked up the small brown bottle, poured some of the viscous, aromatic oil in Loraine's hands and some in her own—they rubbed it all over Bone's glowing skin as he grimaced and twitched.

Loraine glanced at Fiona. "Smells like cloves, cinnamon, frankincense, an' peppermint."

Fiona grinned. "Among other things...It helps in the purification process."

They finished and crawled back through the opening.

The Shaman directed Bone to sit on one of the deerskins, while he sat on the other. He handed him the terra-cotta bowl of brownish liquid.

Bone sniffed of it and wrinkled his nose. "What's this?"

"You don't want to know...just drink half of it."

Bone rolled his eyes, turned the bowl up and downed half of the thick, pungent, liquid. He almost gagged before handing it back to the Shaman.

Anompoli Lawa drank the remainder, set the bowl down, and took a dipper of the blessed, scented, water, and poured it over several of the rocks. They popped, and hissed as steam boiled toward the top of the lodge. He added more water as the rocks re-heated until the dome was filled with the fragrant steam—they could barely see one another.

Bone rocked back and forth as the powerful hallucinogen took effect. The steam seemed to disappear, but didn't—it just got thicker.

Colored lights began to swirl about in the mist and steam inside the lodge and pulsate to the same rhythm as their heartbeats.

Bone looked around him at the figures he was seeing. One was a young girl in her teens. with long blonde hair, running through the thick woods. Another was a broad-shouldered man, in his forties, running behind her, but turning occasionally and firing his Colt pistol. Tendrils of smoke drifted through the trees.

One of the four men chasing them fell to the ground with a shot to his chest. The other men shouted and returned fire. One of them carried a rifle.

The broad-shouldered man stumbled and dropped to his knees. The girl stopped, screamed, and ran back to help him. He pushed her away and back toward the trail. She protested, but he shook his head and pointed for her to go.

HILDEBRANDT & BEAR DOG

She grabbed the sides of her full skirt again and ran out of sight as he turned to fire his gun once more...

The figures began to fade as the steam slowly dissipated. Bone reached out for the man.

"No..."

§§§

CHAPTER TEN

FAYE SKEAN'S BOARDING HOUSE

Bone fell back as the steam continued to dissipate. *Anompoli Lawa* reached over and touched his knee, the big man sat up and shook his head. The Shaman nodded to the skin-covered opening.

Bone rolled over and crawled through the opening with *Anompoli Lawa* just behind him.

The two men exited out into the moonlit darkness only to be hit with the buckets of ice water Silke and Haven dumped on them from both sides.

Bone bellowed like a wounded bull. He stood there a moment, shaking. "My God, didn't remember it being quite like that." He looked at the Shaman. "What's that for again?"

"To cleanse the soul after the vision quest, my son."

He shook his head. "Lord love a duck. Not clean now, never will be."

Faye and Lucy draped quilts over the shivering men as Bone looked up at the sky—the full moon was getting close to being directly overhead.

He looked at Faye as she pulled the quilt closed in front of him. "How long were we in there?"

She smiled. "A good four hours."

"Jesus, Mary, Joseph, an' all the disciples...Seems like it was only fifteen or twenty minutes."

The Shaman nodded as he snugged the patchwork quilt Lucy had given him tighter around his bony shoulders. "That's the way the sweatlodge works, Bone...time does not exist."

"Did you get the rest of your memory back?"

Bone turned to Fiona and started to speak through his chattering teeth.

"Why don't we go inside so Bone and Winchester can get dressed and warm up?...I'll get the coffee on, plus I made my special carrot cake. Come on, ya'll." Faye turned and walked toward the house.

Bone glanced at the Shaman. "Don't think she h...has to say it t...twice."

The elderly Chickasaw smiled. "Especially with that carrot cake of hers."

"Uh-huh...My f...fav."

Loraine moved up beside Bone. "Well, at least you remember you love her carrot cake."

He chuckled and wiggled his eyebrows a couple of times. "That ain't all, B...Babe."

She stopped for a moment, looked up at the stars overhead, then watched him as he strode barefooted toward the back screen door, holding the quilt tightly around him.

Bone and *Anompoli Lawa* had changed into warm, dry clothes and were sitting at the big dining table with the others. Loraine sat beside him.

Faye served everyone hot coffee and large slices of her carrot cake with a thick coating of sorghum and cream cheese frosting.

Bone cut a large forkful of the delicacy, stuck it in his mouth, and slowly savored the flavor. "Oh, kiss a fat baby. I have died and gone to heaven."

Bear Dog laid his paw on Bone's thigh and looked up at him with pleading blue eyes.

Bone got another forkful and stuck it toward the big wolf-dog's open mouth. He licked his share of the cake and icing off.

"Bone!"

He looked at Loraine. "Well, Babe, he asked politely."

She shook her head. "What I put up with."

Bone leaned down. "Maybe Faye'll let you clean everyone's plate when they're done."

Faye rolled her eyes. "Oh, my Lord in Heaven."

Woof!

"Now lay down, Son."

"How much do you remember, Bone?"

He glanced at the Shaman. "Most everything, Doc...Comin' out of the cave an' seein' the lake was gone. Fishin' with Loraine an' her peein' her pants when she caught a big bass..."

"Bone! Don't tell everything...you big oaf."

"Oh, right. Sorry, Babe. I'll leave out the good parts." He winked at her.

She shook her head. "Thank God for small favors."

"Okay...Then, meetin' up with Lucy, even though she already knew we were here."

They looked at the tiny alien. She shrugged. "Bone and I have a connection. That started in 2014...I felt him when they got here."

Haven looked at her. "Huh?"

"It's a long story." She turned back to the others. "Lisanne came and got me on that wild stallion, Steeldust, when Bone dove in front of Fiona and took that bullet...It's a good thing, too, but I already knew she would since it happened well before 2014 in the future when I first met Bone and Loraine."

Haven and Bodie looked at each other, both pinched the bridge of their noses and slightly crossed their eyes.

Lucy giggled.

"Remember meetin' Teddy Roosevelt in the Kiamichi Mountains an' watchin' the sasquach fight with the panth..."

Faye looked at Bone. "The what?"

"*Lofa*, my dear. Hairy man of the forest."

"Thank you, Winchester."

"Then takin' care of the folks killin' Mason's posse, an'..." He pecked Loraine on the cheek. "Me an' my little babe gettin' married in Faye's back yard with Bass Reeves an' everybody here...Goin' on the joint honeymoon to San Antonio with Fiona an' Mason." He grinned an' shook his head. "My great grandparents."

Fiona wagged her finger at him. "Far enough, Bone."

He chuckled. "I know...Findin' the gold statue an' then goin' to Santa Fe, findin' the Anasazi...fightin' with the Skinwalkers, an' meetin' those *sasquach, Auk* an' *Ean*, with *Dalia Marrh*...Comin' back here through that portal thing an' findin' the Spanish gold in the Red Canyon with Butch Cassidy an' the Sundance Kid...Huh, say we'd been busy...Think I got it all."

Bone turned to Loraine and winked at her. She backhanded him across the chest and raised one eyebrow in a not too subtle warning.

"Well, what about Jip Coltrane?...Anything?"

Bone glanced at the Shaman, then at Flynn and nodded. "Best I can tell, Mason, we saw him an' his fifteen-year old daughter in some dense woods with smoke driftin' through the trees...looked like the Kiamichis to me...They were runnin' from some men. Coltrane was firin' at 'em an' they were shootin' back."

He took a breath and looked at *Anompoli Lawa* again. "Don't know if it already happened...or is goin' to."

"Like I said earlier, Bone, there is no past, present, or future in a vision quest."

Padrino took a sip of his coffee. "The scientist, Albert Einstein, will say in twenty years or so from now as part of his theory of Special Relativity...'the past, present, and future all exist at the same time'."

Anompoli Lawa nodded. "I would say, according to our beliefs...he's right."

Bone shrugged. "Guess we'll find out when we get there."

"Need any help? Annabel took the twins to see their grandparents in Alabama."

He turned to Bodie and shook his head. "Out of your jurisdiction, Ranger."

"What about me, Bone?"

He glanced at Flynn and shook his head. "Don't think so, Mason. Looks like we'll be travelin' fast an' light." Bone caught Loraine's eyes. "Be leavin' at daylight an' you'd have to go get your gear back at the ranch...Me, Loraine, Hildebrandt, Bear Dog, an' Sweet Face'll catch the east bound to Clarksville, then north across the Red River by horseback to the Seven Devil Hills in the Choctaw Nation."

He looked down at the black paw on his leg and the two sky blue eyes looking up at him.

"Yes, of course you're going, big guy."

Flynn took a bite of his carrot cake. "Think that's where they are?"

"That was the feelin' I got when we watched them run through the woods, Mason." He looked across the table at *Anompoli Lawa.*

"As did I, Bone...I'm sure I recognized a cave in a ridge they were near."

Lucy smiled. "Follow your intuition...or as you would say, trust your gut."

"Is that one of your Gibb's rules, Bone?"

He shook his head. "Nope, Silke, that one's mine. Followed it since I was in the Corps...Served me well. Learned to never question it."

Loraine smiled. "Watched him do it for years. The rest of what I call a Boneism, is...'Every step you take questioning your gut takes you one step away from what's right'."

Fiona nodded. "That's Bone."

GAINESVILLE DEPOT

"What time do you think we'll get there?"

"Give or take...'bout three this afternoon."

They had worn their tailor-made trail doeskin pants and tops, with tall Apache-style moccasins that Fiona's grandmother made for them—saved carrying extra clothing.

Bear Dog padded alongside Bone as they walked down the aisleway to some open seats facing each other. The wolf-dog would get one entire side to lay down on.

The car lurched as the engine started up and chugged its way from the red brick depot toward the east into the early morning sunrise on the Santa Fe line.

They passed three men, in western garb and wearing side arms, seated on the opposite side of the car.

Bear Dog made a low rumbling growl as they went by.

The men glared at the giant wolf-dog, then at Bone and Loraine as they sat down.

Bear Dog didn't have to jump, he literally stepped up into his seat and promptly laid down—never took his eyes from the three hard cases.

Loraine leaned over to Bone. "Trouble."

He grinned and nodded. "'With a capital T'...an' this is not even River City...as the song from that musical goes...Bear Dog nailed 'em before we did."

"Noticed...Always pay attention when he doesn't like someone."

"Uh-huh."

§§§

CHAPTER ELEVEN

CLARKSVILLE, TEXAS

Tendrils of steam still drifted from the relief valves on the side of the coal-fired locomotive as Bone, Loraine, and Bear Dog stepped to the wooden plank platform.

HILDEBRANDT & BEAR DOG

The three men glanced at them as they disembarked from the train just afterward and walked past the station, headed toward the downtown of the small, agrarian, northeast Texas community.

Bone nodded to them and leaned down to Loraine. "Not the last we've seen of those jackanapes."

"Thinkin' the same thing. Funny thing, being in law enforcement for a while...get to where you can smell the bad guys."

"Uh-huh."

They walked on down to the livestock pens at the rear of the train to get Hildebrandt and Sweet Face.

The second man in the trio, Lou, looked back away from Bone, Loraine, and Bear Dog. "Wonder who the hell they are...them an' 'specially that black wolf-lookin' beast with 'em was givin' us the stink-eye...Mind they're law?"

The leader, Harper, shook his head. "Don't know, don't care...We're headed to the Nations, soon's we meet up with the big man to guide us in."

The smallish third man, Ames, finally turned from also watching them walk down to the corrals. "Shore don't dress like lawdogs...Whoever they be, ain't stayin' in town. Gittin' they horses, I'd say...Headin' out s'mers."

Harper glanced over at him. "Recommend you put what little brains you got into what we gotta do instead of worrin' 'bout strangers dressed in buckskins."

Ames shrugged. "Just sayin's all."

"Less talkin', more thinkin'."

"Yer the boss."

"No, but I'll do till we meet up with 'im."

"Looks like our friends were real interested in where we went."

HILDEBRANDT & BEAR DOG

Loraine glanced over at Bone. "We do present somewhat of a spectacle."

He chuckled, "You think?...Mutt an' Jeff an' their sidekick?"

She backhanded him across the chest. "Bear Dog doesn't like being called a 'sidekick'."

Woof.

"What makes you think I was talkin' 'bout him?"

"Damn you, Bone, don't start with me...You'd wish you still had that amnesia stuff."

He giggled as they walked up to the hostler at the corral next to the livestock car.

Hildebrandt and Sweet Face were already tied to the railing on the outside of the corral. Both were pawing the ground impatiently, tired of being cramped up in the car for eight hours.

Bone and Loraine waited while the hostler unloaded three more horses and a pack mule down the cleated ramp.

"Nickel says they belong to our friends."

"Uh-huh, no bet...Gut says they're goin' to be headed north, too."

"Agree...Most likely in the morning."

"That's a good thing...We should be able to get to *Gloves Fork* on the other side of the *Red* before we have to camp."

"We'd better get a hurry on, then."

"Uh-huh."

Bone flipped the colored hostler a Morgan silver dollar. "Much obliged."

The elderly hostler snatched the coin from the air, looked at it for a second before his eyes went wide. "Thankee, sir, thankee kindly...They been feed an' watered 'fo I unloads 'em...Figured ya'll'd ridin' 'em off."

"Figured good...Sure they appreciated the grain."

"Yasser...did."

Bone and Loraine checked their cinches, then mounted and trotted off toward the north. Bear Dog loped out in front of them.

HILDEBRANDT & BEAR DOG

They rode up to the chain-barge ferry that crossed the *Red River* north of Clarksville and dismounted at the landing.

A grizzled, bearded, old man spat a long stream of viscous, brown tobacco juice, wiped his chin whiskers with the sleeve of his very dirty, faded, blue denim shirt and squinted at them.

"Made m' last run of the day, folks, Come back in the mornin'."

Bone looked across the two-hundred yard wide river. "What do you charge to cross, Old Timer?"

"Old Timer is it? Who you callin' old? My mama called me Jethro Davis when she was mad at me...but usually she'd just call me fer supper." He cackled, slapped his thigh and spat toward the river. "Good'un, wadn't it?...He-he-he. Call me fer supper."

"Yeah, a real knee-slapper. Just an expression, friend...How much do you charge?"

"Dollar a head, animal an' folks...when I run."

"Give you two dollars if you'll make one more run, now."

"Not none of them damnyankee paper dollars?"

Bone shook his head, took a ten dollar Liberty gold coin from his *parfleche* and dropped it from his right into his left palm and held it out.

The old man's jaw dropped and he reached for Bone's palm only to have him close his big hand before he could grab the gold.

"When we get to the other side."

The ferry master looked up at Bone for a moment, then at a grinning Loraine and Bear Dog. "Well, hells-bells, pilgrims, what'er ye waitin' fer...git them beasties on me boat. I'll be pushin' off."

The old ferry operator had chosen the most narrow part of the river in over a half-mile in either direction—a sharp bend where the channel ran to the north, then back to the east before turning south.

The *Red River* was subject to change with each spring flood as was evident by the number of oxbow lakes on both sides—the *Red* tended to meander back and forth over the *Red River* valley.

Bone and Loraine led Hildebrandt and Sweet Face on board. Bear Dog trotted alongside the big black horse.

"By jing, ye got ye some group. Just about the biggest ridin' hoss I ever seed, an' that..." He pointed at Bear Dog. "Looks like must be wolf er somethin'."

"Is...half anyway, with some dog an' maybe a touch of snappin' turtle...or possibly alligator." Bone grinned. "But all man-killer."

"Don't say?"

"Did."

"Uh-right."

The operator cast off toward the Choctaw Nation. He grabbed the top of the big windlass at the front and started the rotation, pulling the barge across the river.

"Need any help with that?"

"Sonny, been turnin' this thing since ye was in diapers...Didn't need no help 'fore ye got here an' won't need none when yer gone...so mind yer manners."

"Right." Bone grinned at Loraine.

The trip took almost thirty minutes before Jethro bumped the nose against the landing. He undid the cable across the front and laid the boarding plank from the deck to the bank.

"Yer in Choctaw country, now, pilgrims. Don't have to worry 'bout yer hair, they be peaceable...fer the most part." He spat another long stream into the murky river. "Be advised to stay outta the Seven Devils, though...'specially this time of year."

Loraine looked at Bone, then back at him. "Oh, why's that?"

Jethro glanced around. "Why, Lassie, don't ye know? They's gonna be a blue moon come All Hallows Eve...only happens ever twenty years er so. There'll be haints comin' out fer shore...Seven Devil Mountains 'er hainted anyways...so the Injuns say."

SEVEN DEVIL MOUNTAINS

A broad-shouldered, square-jawed, forty-year old man crawled quietly on his belly through the brush toward a cave in the side of a ridge.

The late afternoon sun was settling on the rolling hills on the west side of the Choctaw Nation.

The hatless man eased silently up to the edge of a camp set outside the naturally-formed opening in the granite outcrop and peered through the bottom branches of a dense cedar tree.

He counted the men sitting around the campfire drinking coffee. *Seven of the freebooters...not too bad.*

His steely, gray-eyes searched the area, then fell on a set of bare ankles and small feet showing out of the dark shadows just inside the opening.

Ah...gottcha. That bunch of curly wolves are gonna rue the day they messed with the Coltranes.

GLOVES FORK CREEK

Bone glanced to the west at the golden disk disappearing beneath the horizon as Hildebrandt and Sweet Face waded up out of the clear, four-foot deep creek.

Bear Dog shook vigorously to remove the water from his fur when he got up on the bank and immediately scouted the area for rabbit scent.

He turned to Loraine. "Well, Baby Cakes, made it just in time." Bone looked to the east as the top edge of the waning gibbous moon was just peeking over the foothills. "As they said in *Star Wars*...'The force is with us'. Maybe we can take care of business before that blue moon...an' Holloween."

Loraine giggled as she dismounted. "My, my, Bone...Are you superstitious?"

"What? Me?...Ha, naw, Babe." He shook his head. "Think being superstitious is bad luck."

§§§

CHAPTER TWELVE

GLOVES FORK CREEK

Bone stood at the edge of the campfire light staring out into the moonlit darkness.

Loraine glanced up from the log she was sitting on, drinking her second cup of coffee. "What are you lookin' for, spooks?"

He looked back at her. "Huh?...Oh, no, Sweet Pea, just thought I heard somethin'."

"Uh-huh." She patted Bear Dog on the head—he was laying by her feet. "He didn't. So, I wouldn't bother. Got a lot better hearin' an' sense of smell than you or I ever thought about."

Bone turned back and stepped toward the fire. "Uh, right. Knew that...but maybe ghosts don't have a scent an' what if animals can't see 'em?" He glanced back over his shoulder once more.

"He could see Ol' Pike...You, me, Butch, Sundance, an' Fiona all saw...an' talked with him an' he's been dead almost a hundred years...an' besides we're not even to the Seven Devils yet."

"Yeah, I know, but he was different...Besides, was just uh...checkin' things out's all."

"Uh-huh...You forget I've known you for over eight years, Bone. I can read you like a book."

He stared at her a moment, chuckled, then bent down, picked up the hot coffee pot with one of his deerskin gloves and filled his cup before he sat down.

"What were you laughin' at?"

"Oh, back in Jacksboro when you threw me on my ass, then sat on my chest an' I told you my life story."

"Uh-huh."

"An' I sang some of that Carl Dobkins song, *My Heart is an Open Book*?"

Loraine smiled. "All while I was sittin' on your chest...Probably one of the most romantic things you've ever done."

"What do you mean, 'one of the'? I thought it *was* the most romantic thing I'd done...Somethin' I'd never done before, to anyone...ever."

"I know...Are you fixing to get all amorous an' gushy on me?"

"Well?...Would you like for me to?"

HILDEBRANDT & BEAR DOG

Her eyes rolled up. "Damn you, Bone, sometimes you can be so slow."

He sat his cup down and scooted over beside her. "Don't have to hit me with a 2x4 but once."

"We are alone."

Bone pointed at Bear Dog watching them.

"Except for him...an' he tells."

"Bear Dog...Don't watch."

The big wolf-dog immediately snapped his head toward the darkness and laid it between his paws. His cut his eyes briefly at Bone and Loraine embracing before returning forward. His trademark smile crept across his muzzle.

SEVEN DEVIL MOUNTAINS

A cantaloupe-sized rock bounced several times before coming to rest near the fire.

One of the men nearest the fire jumped up from his blanket. "What th' hell?"

The rest of the gang also were quick to hit their feet from their blankets, guns in hand. The first man had also drawn his and tried to peer out into the darkness past the firelight—illuminated only by the light of a gibbous moon shining through the foliage overhead.

Another of the men looked around. "Where'd that come from?"

Carson, the first man, pointed above the cave opening. "There som'ers."

A third man also tried to see out into the darkness. "Ain't no way. Cain't git up there...too steep."

The second man glanced around the camp. "Hey, wher's Curtis?"

"He was right there in his soogan just a bit ago." Carson walked over to Curtis' crumpled blanket. "Everthin's of his is still here...'cludin' his Colt."

Slim looked around. "Reckon he walked out in the brush to take a leak?"

"Curtis!"

There was no response. The remaining six men looked at each other.

Williams, the third man, threw two more logs on the fire. Sparks crackled and swirled up into the night air.

Carson looked at him. "What'd you do that for?"

"Didn't you feel that cold breeze come through right after that rock hit?"

"Oh, right, yeah, now that you mention it...What in hell's goin' on?" He stepped closer to the blazing fire and held his hands out to feel the warmth.

Coltrane noticed the rock arching through the air from above the cave—he could see better than the men around the fire because he hadn't been staring at the flames as most would be doing. *There's nothin' up there.*

Jip had moved back a little from his original location—still close enough to keep an eye on the camp. He pulled his jacket tighter around him against the sudden chill in the night air.

GLOVES FORK CREEK

Bone walked back into camp as the sun was peeking up at the eastern horizon while the moon settled toward the western. He buttoned the top deer antler button on his doeskin pants.

"Is it coffee yet?"

"Just about. Into the second boil now...get your cup."

He picked it up and pitched the last night's left over out to the fire where it sizzled on a log and then he kissed Loraine on the cheek. "Morin', Sugar Babe."

"Mornin'...Aren't you goin' to wash that cup?"

"What for? Just gonna put more coffee in it."

She shook her head. "Like a child."

Bear Dog trotted back into camp with a limp cottontail in his mouth.

Bone glanced at him. "Dang, Son, you went out for breakfast early." He looked at Loraine. "Still waitin' on mine."

"Better hush before you get into trouble."

He giggled.

RED RIVER

The three men from the train pulled rein at the ferry. The old operator making ready for the day looked up as Harper stepped down.

"Gittin' ready to make a run Old Timer?"

Jethro glared at him and spat a stream of tobacco juice in the river. "Naw, pilgrim, was just bored an' needed somethin' to do 'fore the nabobs go to showin' up."

"What's the fee to cross?"

"Dollar a head...horses, too."

"Kinda high, ain't it?"

"Depends on if you an' yer bunch kin swim er not...Current ain't all that bad...might make it 'cross 'fore it takes you to Shreveport, if'n yer lucky...yer choice." He spat again.

There was a low, morning fog drifting across the river and the surrounding bottom. The shore on the Choctaw Nation side was barely visible.

Harper glanced at the murky water and fog, frowned, reached in his pocket for a five dollar gold piece and a silver dollar and handed them to the old man.

"Here. When do we leave?"

"Ya'll kin leave whenever ye've a mind to, I'm leavin' in five minutes."

"Got kind of a smart mouth don'tcha?"

"Depends...I got the ferry, ya'll got squat." He turned and removed the cable barrier to the barge. "Yer goin'...best git aboard me ship."

He turned and nodded at the others, then led his horse down the plank to the center of the flat-bottomed barge. "Cranky old bastard."

Jethro looked up from hooking the cable back. "How's that?"

"Nothin'."

"Uh-huh...What I thought."

Lou turned to Harper. "Reckon how's come the big boss ain't comin'...jest give us that map?"

"What he hired us for...'sides got the feelin' he knows this Coltrane feller...er the other way 'round."

SEVEN DEVIL MOUNTAINS

Coltrane rubbed his arms against the morning chill and peered longingly at the fire. The one called Ezzard stirred the bacon in the cast iron skillet and added a can of beans to it.

The smells of the boiling coffee and sizzling bacon wafting his way on the morning breeze made Jip's mouth water.

He reached in his pocket, took out a strip of tough beef jerky and chewed off a chunk—then pulled up the canteen laying at his side and took a sip. *Wonder what happened to that one what went missin'?...Was there, then gone.*

GLOVES FORK CREEK

Bone and Loraine saddled up Hildebrandt and Sweet Face, mounted, and nudged them into an easy lope toward the low-silhouetted hills in the distance to the north. Bear Dog took his usual place out in front.

"Remember where that ridge with the cave is?"

"Well, sorta."

"Sorta?"

"Well, yeah. If you'll recall, Pard, all those hills look the same...one reason they're called the Seven Devils, I heard. Think you're at one...but you're at another."

"Joy."

§§§

CHAPTER THIRTEEN

GLOVES FORK CREEK

Harper, Lou, and Ames rode up out of the water on the north side of the creek.

Ames' horse shook so violently to rid himself of excess water, the small man fell from the saddle.

Lou looked behind him as Ames was getting to his feet to remount. "Damn, Ames, cain't you sit a saddle? Er do you need a belt?"

"He surprised me's all. Didn't expect him to shake like he had the Saint Vitus Dance...'sides you ain't all that ag-ile yerself. Seen you fall off a time 'er two, Turdwalker."

"Hell you say?"

Ames brushed the dirt from his pants. "You must have 'bout as short a memory as yer tallywacker."

"You little dried up stump, fixin' to kick yer ass."

"An' God's a possum, too."

"Hey, ya'll knock it off an' looky here." Harper had dismounted and was feeling of the ashes and rocks of an dead campfire with the back of his hand.

"Still warm...Bet it was man-mountain an' his woman with that black beast."

Lou also dismounted and looked around. "I'd say. Looks like they left some firewood, too. Reckon we oughta brew up a pot an' chew on a little jerky fer lunch? 'Bout that time."

"Yeah, that's 'bout like you, Jugbutt, thinkin' 'bout yer stomach rather than our bidness."

"Jugbutt?...That tears it." Lou dropped his reins to the ground and charged at the smaller man.

Ames dropped his an' met Lou about halfway.

Harper shook his head. "Not again."

The two men almost butted heads, but managed to grab hold of each other. They hit the ground wrestling, biting, gouging, and slugging—most of their efforts missed.

"Gonna beat you half to death, you little runt!"

"Never have...never will." Ames squirmed over on top and commenced whaling away on Lou's head with both fists. Then he dove down and latched on to his ear with his teeth.

"Ow! Ow! Ow! That's cheatin'!"

"Naw, it's fightin'."

Lou was able to twist over on top of the smaller Ames and did his own pounding with his fists.

Ames managed to get his right leg between Lou's—he brought his knee up sharply, twice.

Lou screamed out, rolled over on his knees, and grabbed his crotch—his forehead pressed against the ground. "Aiiiieeee...ah...ah...ah! Damn you! Not fair."

Ames jumped up with his fists in front of his face dancing around in front of Lou trying to look like John L. Sullivan, but more closely resembled a banty rooster.

"Come on, come on, git up, peckerwood mouth. What's the matter, you let it overload yer jaybird ass?"

Lou wobbled to his feet, his knees together and both hands covering his crotch. His eyes were crossed as he tried to focus on Ames.

"Awright, girls, the dance is over. Ya'll want somethin' to eat an' some

Arbuckles' best git to it. Ain't gonna be here all day."

Lou slowly straightened up pushed down on his abdomen below his gunbelt and shook his finger at Ames. "We'll finish this later, Asswipe."

"What you said last time."

"What'd I just say?" Harper walked over to the two friends turned combatants with both hands on his hips.

ALIKCHI BRANCH

Bone and Loraine splashed Hildebrandt and Sweet Face through the shallow branch just to the south of the Seven Devils after letting them drink their fill.

Bear Dog also paused to lap up some of the cool, clear water before crossing through the branch in three jumps.

"Well, there they are, Baby Doll." Bone swept his arm from west to east. "The Seven Devils, the south side of the Kiamichis."

She nodded. "Yeah, remember now, they do all look the same...like potatoes."

"Some folks call 'em the potato hills in our time...still get lost in there in a heartbeat."

"Let's not be one of those that do."

Bone patted his *parfleche*. "Got my handy-dandy Boy Scout compass right here...Like that card, never go anywhere without it."

"Right, now to figure out where that ridge was or still is."

"Uh-huh. Been ponderin' on that."

"That what you call it?"

"Smart ass."

"So, which way first, Davy?"

"Let's work from west to east since we're closer to the west end...Have to almost be on top of that ridge since it's just below the treetops."

"I know...Your vision didn't give you a better idea?"

"Uh-uh." Bone shook his head. "Could just see trees an' that ridge in the background."

HILDEBRANDT & BEAR DOG

"If we had an airplane or even a drone..."

"An' if the barkin' dog hadn't stopped to pee, he'd of caught the train."

"Yeah, yeah, 'ifs' an' buts don't mean much."

"Nope, just old fashioned cop work, now...on the ground. Doesn't matter what space time-frame we're in."

SEVEN DEVIL MOUNTAINS

Jip Coltrane worked his way around the small clearing to a location closer to the ridge face and the cave.

He couldn't see Alice's naked feet or ankles from his present position—but it was closer.

One of the men went inside the cave with a tin plate of beans and a canteen.

Well, 'least they're feedin' her.

He searched for a spot where he could get even closer. *Need to thin the odds down some.* Jip unsheathed his Bowie from its scabbard and checked the edge. *Even if I...no, when I get her out, it's at least a mile back to my horse. Make do, I guess...Least it's down to six of the miscreants.*

He turned at the noise of horses moving through the trees. *Uh-oh.*

Harper, Lou, and Ames slowly walked their horses single file along a narrow game trail through the woods and emerged into the clearing.

They dismounted in the face of six guns pointed at them.

"Hey, hey, put them shooters away, boys. The big man sent us. Thought maybe should have a few more guns on hand."

Carson stepped forward, still holding his Remington on Harper. "Awright, got names?"

"I'm Harper." He pointed at the others. "That's Lou an' Ames...You'd be Carson?"

"Close enough...Picket your horses over yonder." He pointed to his left. "Slim, show 'em where."

Harper looked at the men. "Thought there were seven of ya'll."

"Was. One disappeared durin' the night...Curtis."

"Disappeared?"

"Yeah, 'nuff said. Now go picket them horses...Ya'll brought more grub an' coffee?"

"Did." He pointed at the cotton poke sacks tied to their saddlehorns.

Carson nodded at Wiley and Ezzard. They walked over and collected the three poke sacks.

Harper and the others followed a tall drink of water named Slim along a different game trail to another grass-covered glen beside a small branch.

Carson turned to the other two, Williams and Ira. "Leastwise, bossman's right, a few more guns cain't hurt." His eyes cut to Ames' horse disappearing down the trail. "Just don't know how handy these bean eaters are."

The biggest man in the bunch, Ira, turned from also watching them vanish down the trail. "'Spect we'll find out...one way or 'nuther."

Coltrane turned and leaned against the trunk of the big hickory. *Damnation, change of plans.* He peered back out around the tree at the camp.

He then worked his way from the camp to a small spot he'd picked so he could reconnoiter. *Nine, now...Wonderful.*

Jip sat down, leaned against a large red oak, took several pieces of jerky from a pouch hung around his neck and shoulder.

He tore a strip off with his strong white teeth and chewed thoughtfully. *What the Sam Hill happened to that guy they called Curtis? Is there anything there I can take advantage of?...Come on, man, think. One against nine...tough row to hoe. Need an edge.*

§§§

CHAPTER FOURTEEN

SEVEN DEVILS

Slim led Harper and his men into the glade where they stripped the gear from their horses and picketed them on some lush grass after letting them water at the stream.

Harper stepped up to the tall, skinny man. "You got any idea what we're doin' here?"

"Well, kinda. Tell you what I know on the way back to camp."

The trail to the horse glade from camp went underneath a huge hickory tree near the edge.

Slim led the others, as they carried their saddles and soogans, back toward camp.

He glanced over his shoulder at Harper. "We've got this fifteen year old gal in a cave by the camp. The bigman has sent a note to her daddy, seems the family has a bucket load of money...plus knows where this copper box of gold...Dang, where'd that come from?" The skinny man shivered.

Ames, just behind Slim, pulled his jacket tighter around him against a sudden chilling of the breeze through the woods.

Harper and Lou did the same.

"Brrrr."

Slim looked quickly around as he shivered and wrapped his arms about himself. "Uh-oh."

A body abruptly dropped from the branches directly over the game trail in front of him. It jerked to a stop, swinging back and forth, the boots on the man were three feet from the ground. A rope was tied around his neck—the missing man, Curtis.

Slim fell back on his butt as the four men screamed almost in unison. The one nearest the swinging, spinning body, Slim, was the loudest.

The skinny man scrambled to his feet and sprinted down the trail toward base camp.

Harper, Lou, and Ames dropped their saddles and were right on Slim's heels— running like their hair was on fire, screaming every step.

Jip spun around at the first scream and scrambled quietly through the undergrowth back toward his spot closer to the camp. He noticed an abrupt chill in the air. *Cold air Again. Wonder where that's comin' from?*

Bone bumped Hildebrandt to a halt. "Listen, Babe, hear that?"

Loraine cocked her head. "Sounds like echoes...Almost have to be comin' from that direction." She pointed toward the east and the balance of the Seven Devils.

She and Bone were in the valley between the westernmost hills.

There were five in a line east and west and two more immediately to the south of the line on the west side—it looked somewhat like the outline of a large pan or dipper.

"Stopped now." He looked at Loraine. "Sure sounded like men yellin' to me, didn't it you?"

"It did." She looked at him. "You're cogitatin' aren't you?"

"Am...My gut says go east young man, go east."

"Think that was Horace Greeley that said 'Go west, young man, go west'."

Bone shrugged. "Literary license." He looked down at Bear Dog. "Find, Son, find." He pointed east.

The giant wolf-dog spun about and took off through the woods to the east.

"Think he knows what to look for?"

"He knows." Bone nudged Hildebrandt to the east with his left knee. "Just as well work that way."

Loraine looked at the tree covered, undulating hills to the east as she turned Sweet Face that way also. "Into the lion's den...Where's Daniel?"

"He's findin' the lions for us."

"I know."

Coltrane watched as the four panicky men ran breathlessly into camp.

Carson was on his feet, coffee cup still in his hand as they stumbled to a stop near the fire. They turned as one to look back down the trail into the woods.

"What's wrong with ya'll?"

Lemual added a log to the fire to combat the sudden chilly air.

"Curtis! Saw Curtis!" Slim bent over with his hands on his knees trying to catch his breath. "Saw 'im!"

"So? Where is he?" Carson looked around the four frightened men at the trail behind them.

Slim pointed behind him. "Hangin'...hangin' from that big hickory back yonder."

"Dead?"

Slim and the others nodded.

"As you can git." Slim took a deep breath. "Dropped out of the tree as we walked...walked under it."

Carson nodded to Ezzard and Wiley. "Check it out."

The two men exchanged nervous glances.

"Today, you idiots!"

They grabbed their Winchesters from their bedrolls and walked tentatively down the narrow path.

"You tellin' me he dropped out of that tree when ya'll were walkin' back? Wadn't there when you walked in?"

"That's right, Boss. Wadn't there, then wus...Like to have dropped right on top of me."

"Bull...You got some Who-Hit-John on you?"

Slim voraciously shook his head. "Uh-uh...Damn shore wish I did, though."

Carson frowned.

Ezzard and Wiley strode back into camp and directly up to Carson.

"Nothin' there, Boss."

Wiley nodded. "That's right, nothin' atall, no body, no rope...Wadn't nothin' 'ceptin' their saddles an' gear layin' in the trail."

"Then what the hell did they see?"

Harper stepped forward. "Swear to God, Carson, a body dropped right out of that big ass tree. Was still swingin' back an' forth when we hauled it outta there...Didn't know who it was 'till Slim tol' you it was a guy named Curtis...But he was damn sure there."

Ames and Lou nodded.

"That's right...was."

Ames turned and backhanded Lou across the chest. "Knocked me down runnin' outta there, big sissy."

"Sissy? You little squirt, yer not big enough to see."

"Big enough to kick yer ass...Damn galoot."

Lou shoved the little man. "Not in this lifetime."

"Awright, knock it off...Gonna tie you two inside a cotton sack an' leave you." Harper turned to Carson. "This Curtis fella...the one what went missin'?"

"Yeah."

"Turned cold then too." Lemual rubbed his arms.

Harper looked at the man dressed in bib overalls an' a canvas jacket.

"Like just a few minutes ago?"

Lemual nodded and looked nervously around at the forboding woods.

"Choctaw say these hills is got haints."

Carson glared at Wiley. "Hogsnot!"

"Well, shore don't see no redhides in here nowheres."

Coltrane leaned his back against the big red oak. *Could be the change I need. Captain Flynn always said, 'A confused an' frightened enemy is always a good opportunity.'*

He unbuckled his Colt from around his hips, wrapped the gun in his wild rag and looked down at the base of the tree. *Perfect.*

Coltrane pulled his Bowie, hollowed out a slight depression in the dirt against the bole and laid the gun and gunbelt in it with the Bowie on top. He then brushed a thick layer of dead leaves from the forest floor over them and stood back to survey his efforts. *Uh-huh, that'll do...Now's the time.*

He took his Opinel folding knife from his pocket, pulled his pant leg up, dropped it inside the barrel of his boot, and pulled his pant leg back down. Coltrane smiled, turned and strode through the woods directly into the outlaw's camp.

Williams, Carson, Wiley, and Harper saw him at the same time—they all drew their guns—Ames, Lou, Ezzard, Ira and Slim followed suit.

Coltrane held both hands over his head as he walked in. "Not carryin', boys...I'm your huckleberry."

A pair of blue eyes watched the men in the clearing around the campfire. Bear Dog backed away from under the dogwood tree, turned and loped away, back to the west.

§§§

CHAPTER FIFTEEN

SEVEN DEVILS

"Wonder how far he had to go to find someone?" Loraine eased Sweet Face back into a walk from the single-foot they had been using traveling east.

Bone shrugged. "Far as it takes. He knows he's lookin' for those voices."

"How does he know?"

"Magic."

"Damn you, Bone...never a straight answer."

"Oh, every once in a while...*Acushla*."

"Now, dammit, there you go. Every time I try to get on you, something comes out of your mouth that melts me...like *Acushla*."

He grinned. "Well, that lady, Lollie, on the stagecoach that time you got shot? She heard me talkin' to you while you were unconscious in my lap an' told me you were my *Acushla*. Asked her what that meant an' she said it was Irish for, 'pulse of my heart'...Seemed like the thing to say."

Loraine shook her head and wiped a tear from her eye. "See, that's what I mean."

Hildebrandt's ears flicked forward—he chuckled, then whinnied.

Bone focused where the big horse was looking and spotted movement in the woods up ahead. "Looky yonder."

Loraine turned her head and saw Bear Dog loping around a bend in the game trail in their direction.

"That didn't take long."

Bone chuckled. "Like Ricky Nelson used to say on the old *Ozzie an' Harriet Show,* in the '50s...'I don't mess around, boy'."

"Before my time."

"Mine too...Reruns. But, that's what Bear Dog would say if he could talk."

"He can almost talk as it is."

"I know...Gets mad when we don't pay attention."

The big wolf-dog stopped in the middle of the trail, looked at Bone, then Loraine, spun around with a *woof,* and took off back the way he'd come.

Bone glanced at Loraine. "If that's not talkin', don't know what is."

They eased Hildebrandt and Sweet Face into an amble trot to keep up with Bear Dog.

"Daddy!"

Jip turned and looked up at the cave opening. Alice stood just inside, her right arm was waving at him. He could see a rope tied around her ankle.

Coltrane ground his jaws together and turned his steel-gray eyes on Carson with a look that would melt granite.

"If you scum-suckers harmed one hair on my daughter's head...this world's not big enough for you to hide in." His upper lip raised up in a snarl. "God as my witness...I'll hunt every last mother's son of you down." He lowered his right hand a little and pointed at Carson. "Startin' with you...We all have a beast inside us. I've seen mine...trust me, you don't want to...it won't be pretty...Understand me?"

Carson held up his hands. "Easy now, Coltrane, nobody's touched her...she's fine. For now."

"Now or later, don't matter whose fault, you remember what I said...Get that rope off her leg an' let her go. You've got me."

"Well, now, not just yet...Don't have what we want."

"Which is?"

"Understand you know where Captain T.M.'s big copper box with $80,000 in gold coin is."

Coltrane laughed under his breath. "You believe that old wives' tale?"

Carson stared at Coltrane for a long moment. "Point is, your daughter remains safe, but with us, until we see that gold...clear enough?...Or do I have to draw a picture in the dirt for you?"

Bone bumped Hildebrandt to a stop and sniffed the air. "Campfire nearby." He pointed upslope of the third hill in the line of five. "That way...upwind a little ways."

Bear Dog had sat down on his haunches watching Bone, then he got up and followed them off the trail.

"Best we leave the horses here an' go in on foot...looks like there's a branch over yonder with some open areas."

"Bone, isn't that a red roan horse through the trees there?"

"Believe you're right, Babe."

They dismounted and led Hildebrandt and Sweet Face through the woods toward the roan horse.

"He's been picketed out here close to the water."

Bone looked around, then led Hildebrandt up close enough that he could take a look at the roan's tack. He examined the saddle. The horses nickered at each other.

"I'd say that's a JC brand on the corner of the short-skirt, wouldn't you, Pard?"

Loraine stepped closer to examine the tooled four-inch high initials in the leather. She nodded.

"Believe you're right. Wonder what JC stands for?"

Bone nodded. "Try Jip Coltrane on for size."

"Oh, right."

"Campfire nearby, maybe a mile or less...horse staked out, pretty well hidden...I'd say the former cavalry officer is doin' some reconnoiterin'."

"Pretty good guess, Bone."

He shook his head. "Uh-uh, Babe, no guess to it...Looks like somethin' I'd do an' somethin' we're gonna do right behind him."

He picketed Hildebrandt and loosened his girth. Loraine did the same with Sweet Face. They were both able to reach the water like the roan.

Bone glanced up through the trees to the west at the sun settling toward the horizon.

"Be dark in a bit an' that's a good thing."

"You say so."

"Uh-huh...work better in the dark."

"Easy for you to say."

"Just stick with me, Kid...Bear Dog, lead out, Son."

They moved through the trees toward the ridge to the north.

"Awright, git in there with yer daughter. Be somebody right outside, 'case yer wonderin'." Wiley turned and headed back down the slope to the camp.

Coltrane watched the outlaw work his way down and nod to Lemual.

The bib overall clad gang member picked up his Winchester and headed up toward the cave.

Jip smiled and turned to Alice. "You all right, Honey?"

He couldn't hug her because they had tied his hands behind his back with a narrow strip of latigo. But only her leg was secured by a hemp rope tied to a large rock—she wrapped her arms around his neck.

"Oh, Daddy, thank you for coming. What are we going to do?"

"You knew I would, Baby, you knew I would."

She wiped the tears from her cheeks and nodded.

He glanced at the opening to make sure Lemual wasn't in hearing distance yet. "Don't worry, we'll get out of this."

"I know. I've just been so scared."

"I'm so sorry you got pulled into this."

"Do you know where that box is?"

Jip looked at the opening again and watched Lemual sit down just outside with his back against the cliff face.

He winked at Alice and sat down himself against the side of the cave.

She sat beside him. "This looks like an old mine, Daddy."

"It was, Hon…Silver mine, operated by our family back in the mid 1800s."

"Really?"

He nodded as he watched the shadows of the gloaming getting longer outside.

Darkness comes quickly in the mountains when the sun disappears behind the horizon.

Down in the camp, Coltrane could see Wiley throw a couple of limbs on the fire. Sparks swirled up into the early night air, then abruptly the fire went completely out like it was on a switch.

Several of the men close by, jumped to their feet with shouts.

"Hey, hey! What in hell? What'd you do, Wiley?"

"Didn't do a damn thing, just throwed some more wood on the fire cause of 'nother of one of them cold breezes come through."

Carson and the others looked around for anything else happening.

He handed Wiley a tube of matches. "Git that lit again...can't see squat."

Wiley stripped some phloem and cambium from the inside of a slab of dry cottonwood bark and rubbed it between his palms until it was almost a powder. He stuck the wad just under one of the previously burning logs and held a burning match to it.

HILDEBRANDT & BEAR DOG

The tinder caught quickly, flamed up and spread to the limbs and sticks on above it. Flames soon were blazing and light once again illuminated the campsite.

Carson turned to the others. "Everbody here?"

Harper nodded. "My guys are all here."

Slim glanced at the other group. "Looks like everbody's here but Lemual, Carson, an' he's up to the cave."

"Yeah, too dark up there to see...Williams, go up there an' check."

"Right, Boss."

He loosened his Colt in the holster, grabbed a burning branch from the fire, and worked his way up the slope to the cave.

Williams held the torch over his head when he reached the cave. "Lemual, where you be, boy?" There was no answer.

He stuck his head inside the cave and saw Coltrane and his daughter were sitting in the dark against the rock wall.

"Where's Lemual?"

Coltrane looked up at him. "Beats me, was out there before that campfire went out...He not now?"

"No." Williams turned and hurried back down to the camp.

"He's gone, Boss. Just like Curtis...Just vanished in thin air." Williams held up a Winchester and bag of tobacco. "Left his rifle an' *Bull Durham* smokes."

Carson looked around at the darkness. "What the hell's goin' on?"

§§§

CHAPTER SIXTEEN

SEVEN DEVILS

Coltrane watched the men grouped around the blazing fire at the camp down below. He turned to his daughter.

"Hon, pull up my right pant leg to above my boot top an' reach down inside...My foldin' knife is in there."

Alice took her breath in sharply as her eyes widened. "Oh, we're going to slip out of here?"

He nodded in the dark. "Good a time as any. They're confused an' frightened...plus there's no one outside guarding the cave, right now...Quickly."

She grabbed the bottom of his right jeans pant leg and pulled it up over the top of his black stovepipe cavalry-style boots.

She reached down inside. "What do you think happened to the man that was outside guarding the cave?"

"No idea, Honey. Could be he got tired of those guys down there an' took off."

"But why would he leave his rifle and smokin' tobacco?" Alice held up his knife.

"Good point...Guess it's possible that the old legends I heard from the Choctaw when we lived here when I was almost your age."

"Which was?"

"They believed these mountains were haunted...an' they got the stories from the Caddo before them...Maybe spooks got him...Go ahead an' open that."

Alice used her thumbnail and pried the largest of the two blades open. "Do you believe in ghosts an' spirits?"

"Well, I believe there has to be something to those old legends or they wouldn't still be around...Philosophers an' historians say that myths an' legends all have a seed of truth in them." He turned with his back to her. "Cut those leather straps...Try not to get me, that thing's razor sharp."

"I know. Watch you sharpen it after every time you use it."

"Knife's not much good if it's not sharp...That's it, Honey, you got it."

Jip pulled his hands apart and the rest of the latigo fell to the floor of the cave. He rubbed his wrists to restore the circulation, then reached for his knife.

She handed it to him, handle first like she'd been taught, he quickly cut the rope around her ankle—closed the blade, dropped the knife back in his boot, and pulled the cuff down.

"Guess they took your shoes?"

"Uh-huh...They're down in the camp somewhere."

"Have to stay there...I'll carry you."

Loraine leaned over close to Bone. "What do you think they're upset about?"

He shook his head. "Don't know, but they're right scared about somethin'...Look at 'em, they're all lookin' around at the darkness."

"That's really odd."

"If I had to guess...I'd say it's about spooks." Bone grimaced. "Hate spooks...I'm about spooks like Indiana Jones is about snakes."

"Looks like they are too...What do you think about using that?"

"You mean pretend we're spirits or somethin'?"

"Why not?"

"Oh, boy...Hate this. Like we're temptin' fate or the spirit gods...walkin' on graves...whatever."

"Bear Dog an' I'll protect you."

The big wolf-dog looked up at them.

"Yeah, but what's goin' to protect ya'll?"

Loraine reached down between her ample breasts and lifted up a silver and gold crucifix hung on a gold chain around her neck. "This."

Bone looked up at the almost full blue moon nearing apogee. "With the moonlight, gonna have a lots of good shadows...this may be fun."

"Is that all you think about? Fun? This is serious, Bone, there's a fifteen year old girl to think about."

"Babe, if it ain't fun, it won't come out right...Even serious stuff should be fun."

Loraine shook her head, "Oh, Lord...All right, let's go."

He leaned down to Bear Dog and whispered in his ear. The big guy took off for the camp and circled around the edge, just out of the light from the fire, but close enough to go through the moonlight filtering through the trees.

"Watch, Babe."

"What'd you tell him?"

"Just watch."

Ames turned sharply. "What was that?"

Lou looked back at him. "You see somethin', Little Man?"

"Seen somethin' in the shadows over yonder." He pointed off to the side of camp. "An' don't call me Little Man."

"Huh...If the shoe fits...Jesus, there is somethin' out there."

"What?" Carson looked. "Don't see nothin'."

"Well, there was somethin' out there."

Slim moved closer to the fire. "I seed a shadow movin' over thataway." He pointed halfway around the edge from where Ames did.

The eight men all pulled their shooters and pointed them in various directions at the darker parts of the surrounding woods.

Bone cupped his hands around his mouth and laughed like Dracula from an old black and white horror movie. "Mu-ha-ha-ha-ha-ha."

He nudged Loraine and she screamed like a B movie horror queen.

He leaned over to her as they changed locations. "I just love the old 30s an' 40s black an' white horror movies...*Dracula, Frankenstein, The Wolf Man.*"

"I can tell...I like some of the newer ones, *Halloween* an' *Nightmare on Elm Street.*"

"Yeah, those too."

Ames was the first to pull his trigger, the others soon followed suit. Leaves and shot-in-two branches fell all around the camp from the bullets whizzing through the trees.

"Hold it, hold it." Carson stuck a hand up in the air. "Ain't no good shootin' at what we cain't see."

The panicked men turned to the leader with 'are you sure' looks and quit firing as gunsmoke filled the campsite.

When the shooting began, Coltrane motioned for Alice to jump on his back. She jumped up, wrapped her arms around his neck and her legs about his waist.

"Can't pick a better time than this, Hon."

He slipped out of the cave and worked sideways through the trees along the face of the sloping ridge.

"Need to work around to the far side of the camp. Got Red picketed 'bout a mile or so in that direction."

"Can you carry me that far, Daddy?"

"Honey, I'll carry you as far as I have to. Ground's way too rough for you to run or even walk on barefoot."

Bone and Loraine had flattened out on the ground when the shooting started as some of the wayward shots came close overhead.

Bone giggled softly "Best stay down for a bit, Babe, one of those idiots could get lucky."

"Right."

Coltrane and Alice reached the more level area at the bottom of the ridge and were working their way through the darkness trying not to run into limbs. The shooting had stopped.

They could see the flickering campfire through the foliage and saw a large log fly through the air from the trees. It landed on its end, bounced up, and fell almost on top of the blazing fire.

Sparks and burning branches flew up into the air and scattered in all directions.

Most of the men panicked again and ran into the woods, firing as they did.

One of the men, Ira, running pell-mell along a narrow game trail, ran almost head-on into Coltrane and Alice. The impact knocked the pair off the trail, causing Coltrane to stumble into the brush and whoa-vines at the side of the trail.

Ira struggled back to his feet—pointing his gun in all directions. He could just make out Coltrane and Alice starting to rise in a sliver of moonlight between shadows...

§§§

CHAPTER SEVENTEEN

SEVEN DEVILS

Bone raised his head and peeked at the camp. "Huh...Hey, Babe, they're all gone."

Loraine looked up, also. "They run into the woods?"

"Must have. Scared 'em more than I thought...Wait a minute, one of the yahoos is comin' back into camp an'...uh-oh, I'd say that's Coltrane an' his daughter with him."

"They look like in your vision?"

Bone nodded. "Uh-huh...exactly."

"Well, pretty accurate, so far."

"So far."

The rest of the eight men drifted back into camp and gathered close to the fire.

Carson looked at Ira. "What's the deal with Coltrane an' the girl bein' outta the cave?"

"Run into 'em on that trail over yonder." He pointed back over his shoulder. "Thinkin' this lawdog is meby our haint...'long with the little split-ta..."

Coltrane backhanded Ira across the face before he could finish, knocking him to the ground on his back. His nose was smashed and his lip split wide open—blood sprayed all over the man's face and boiled shirt.

Ira looked up, with blood streaming down his face, and thumbed the hammer back on his Colt.

Coltrane snarled at him. "Disrespect my daughter again, slime bucket...I will end you, guns or no guns."

"Awright, awright, put that away, Ira, you deserved that." Carson turned to Coltrane. "How'd ya'll git outta that cave?"

He shrugged. "Your men must not have done a good job in tyin' us up. Saw everybody leave...figure we would too."

"Well, figured wrong." He turned back to Ira. "If he's our haint, how'd he move them bodies an' why didn't he take Lemual's Winchester? Use your head, man...Now take 'em back up there...an' this time make sure they're tied up. Go help 'im, Slim."

The two men grabbed burning branches each from the fire for torches and led Coltrane and his daughter back up the slope. "Oh, by the way, come mornin' you're gonna show us where that box is."

Coltrane looked back over his shoulder at Carson.

Bone put his Smith and Wesson back into his holster and grinned at Loraine. "Like this guy...Got guts."

"It's his daughter."

"I know, but still that takes guts...Unless he knows something we don't."

"Like what?"

"Beats me, Babe, if I knew that, then he wouldn't know something we don't."

"Do what?"

"Nothin'."

"What do we do now?"

"Keep on keepin' on...till it's time not to keep on."

"Uh-huh...Then?"

"Get 'em outta there..." Bone frowned. "Wonder what that box is that guy mentioned?"

Loraine shook her head. "Must have money or gold in it sounds like."

Bone nodded and looked back at the camp. "Could be...could be." He turned to

Loraine. "Let 'em get settled back down an' roll up in their blankets...I'll slip into their camp later...leave a surprise or two."

"Like back in Red Canyon?"

He raised his eyebrows and grinned. "Maybe so."

Ira shoved Coltrane in the back causing him to fall to his knees inside the cave.

"Daddy! Are you all right?" Alice turned to the tobyman. "You're a horrid man."

"Well, don't know what that word 'horrid' means little lady, but I'm gonna kill him 'fore this is over." He wiped at some of the blood still dripping from his nose.

Coltrane got to his feet. "You'd better be good at it because you'll only get one chance."

"Hey, Ira." Slim held up the latigo. "This here's been cut." He looked at Coltrane. "You had a knife, didn'cha?"

195

"Did I?"

Slim handed his torch to Ira and patted Jip all over, paying special attention to his pockets. "Nothin'...Where is it?"

"Where is what?"

Slim slapped Coltrane across the face. "Don't mess with me...Carson ain't here to bail you out. Now, where's that knife?"

"No idea...musta lost it goin' down the slope. Thought it was in my pocket."

"Yeah." Slim picked up the latigo again, jerked Coltrane's hands behind his back and retied them extra tight. "There, that'll hold you."

"Can't feel my fingers. Might be too tight."

"Ha, that's 'too damn bad', then."

He redid the rope around Alice's ankle and turned to Ira. "I'll take first watch. Have Carson send up somebody to relieve me in a couple hours."

Ira glared at Coltrane, then turned and headed toward the entrance. "Right."

HILDEBRANDT & BEAR DOG

Slim went outside, sat down against the cliff face and rolled a smoke.

The almost full moon was well past apogee when Bone slipped down from their observation spot.

"Come on, Bear Dog, maybe we'll find something for you to do, too."

The two disappeared into the shadows like a pair of wraiths, making no sound whatsoever. Loraine lost sight of them in seconds.

She smiled in the moonlight. "Spooks got nothing on those two."

Even when Bone was in-between the shadows, he was hard to see. His full suit of medium brown doeskins, plus the camo face paint from the kit in his *parfleche* in dark green, light green and brown made him almost invisible—Bear Dog just looked like a shadow.

Bone glanced around the camp at the sleeping figures illuminated by moonlight and occasionally some flickers from the dying campfire. He saw who he was looking for.

He took his Ka-Bar Marine Corps fighting knife, doubled one of his deerskin gloves over the end of the handle to deaden the noise, and thumped Harper hard behind his ear.

The man jerked from the blow, but wouldn't be waking up for a while. Bone drew the razor edge of the Ka-Bar across his neck just deep enough to make it bleed. Next he pulled Harper's knees up and tied his hands together to his ankles with a leather thong from his *parfleche*.

Bone nodded to Bear Dog and pointed to the main poke sack over near the fire. The wolf-dog padded over, grabbed the neck of the cotton sack in his jaws and headed to the woods with it.

Bone systematically took all their handguns, shucked the shells from each, then replaced the empty guns back in their holsters.

He nodded, grinned, and started to ease out of the camp when a chill seemed to envelope the entire clearing. Bone shivered, stopped, stepped back over to the fire and quietly laid three good-sized pieces of blowdown on the coals—he smiled again and slipped out of the camp.

It only took a couple of minutes to get back to where Loraine was waiting.

"Oh! You startled me, Bone, damn you, you always do that."

"Sorry, Babe, I was in my nighttime mode."

He turned to see Bear Dog come in right behind him carrying the heavy poke sack in his mouth with the outlaws main supplies.

"Good boy." He handed Loraine the sack. "Might be some stuff in here we can use...maybe some canned pickled peaches."

"What else did you do?"

Bone glanced over his shoulder through the trees at the camp. The dead blowdown he had put on the fire was blazing up, lighting the entire camp.

Carson was the first to wake up, mainly because he was closest to the fire.

He looked around. "Who put all those logs on the fire?"

The others stirred from their soogans—all except Harper, he was out cold.

"Well, whoever done it, kinda glad. 'Nother one of them cold winds come through." Wiley pulled his blanket around his shoulders.

Slim sat up and glanced at the others.

"I come in just a bit ago when Ira relieved me up to the cave. Fire was down to coals then."

Lou reached over and nudged Harper. 'Hey, wake up."

He didn't move. Lou poked him again. Nothing.

"Somethin's wrong with Harper. He reached over and pulled the man's blanket back. "Hey! He's all tied up."

The others got up out of their bedrolls and looked over at Harper.

"He daid?" Ames leaned over with his hands on his knees, then felt of the darkness under his chin. "Oh, damnation! His throat be cut!"

Carson ran over to the two men. "Hell you say?"

"Carson, Williams is gone!" Ezzard stood over the empty blanket. "Gun an' all his personal stuff's still here." He looked at Carson stepping over. "Jest like the others."

Bone looked at Loraine. "Now that's odd. That guy was there when I left a few minutes ago...before that cold breeze came through."

Loraine raised her eyebrows and mouthed the theme from the *X Files*, "Do-do-do-do."

§§§

CHAPTER EIGHTEEN

SEVEN DEVILS

Ira got to his feet and moved a little to get a better view of the camp to see what the racket was all about.

Coltrane noticed him standing at the edge of the mouth of the cave in the moonlight looking down at the camp.

"Somethin' happenin' down there, Ira?"

"Yeah, don't rightly know what, though...Musta had 'nother of those cold breezes, somebody throwed several logs on the fire."

"What's that chill all about?"

Ira glanced over his shoulder into the darkness of the cave and shook his head. "No idee, jest of a sudden gets cold...an' somebody disappears. Found one of our men, Curtis, hangin' from a tree over the trail to where the horses is...then the body wuz gone...like it never wuz."

A smile crept across Coltrane's face in the dark. "Don't say? Think there's critters out there?...Or reckon it could be spirits?"

"Don't know. Dang shore don't like neither...Ready to get outta here. Place is spooky."

"The Choctaw say evil spirits roam these hills...Why they're called the Seven Devils."

Ira tried to look into the cave. "That fer true?"

"What they believe. These mountains are called the Seven Devils...aren't they?"

"Uh...yeah." Ira did his best to see into the woods around the cave.

"Say there's folks come into these hills..." Coltrane slowly shook his head. "...an' never ever seen again."

"Really?"

"For a fact."

Carson stepped over to get a closer look at the still-unconscious Harper.

Lou pointed at the line of blood on his neck that went from ear to ear. "That there blood is clottin' up...don't reckon he's dead."

Carson felt of Harper's head. "Well, he's got a knot the size of a goose egg back behind his ear...Somebody whacked 'im good, then tried to cut his throat."

Lou looked into the darkness. "Er meby it was somethin'...'stead of somebody an' it might'ov been in a hurry."

Harper groaned and reached his hand up to the spot behind his ear where the knot was. "Oh, wha-happened?...Feels like been kicked in the head by a mule."

Then, he felt of his throat, looked at his hand in the flickering light of the fire and tried to sit up. "Great horny toads, throat's cut!...My God, somebody help me 'fore I bleed plumb to death."

Carson stood up. "You ain't gonna bleed to death, that's just a scratch...mostly."

"Who done it?"

"If you don't know, we sure's hell don't." He looked at the ground a moment. "Need to put somebody on guard for the rest of the night." Carson pointed at Ames. "You take first guard."

"By myself?"

"Yes, you idiot, by yourself...Runnin' out of men...Get yer rifle."

Bone watched the already well-lit camp as one of the men added a couple more dry deadfall logs to the fire as Carson pointed at the smallest man.

"Huh-huh." He grinned. "Puttin' out a guard...Figured he would." Bone glanced at Loraine. "An' there's that chill again."

Bone glanced up at the branches overhead as a dark red black gum leaf drifted to the ground. "Leaves turnin'...Hope the sparks from that bonfire they got goin' don't blow into the woods...They're tinder-dry."

Bear Dog's ears went flat against his head and a soft whine emanated from his throat.

Loraine wrapped her arms about herself. "There doesn't seem to be any wind, really...it just turns cold all of a sudden and something's got Bear Dog upset."

Bone nodded. "Noticed." He looked over at the cotton sack Bear Dog brought in. "Any pickled peaches in there?"

HILDEBRANDT & BEAR DOG

"Haven't looked." Loraine loosened the cord around the top and dug around inside. "Got slab bacon, coffee, canned beans, sugar...ah, here we go." She pitched him a can of pickled peaches.

Bone snatched it from the air and pulled his John Wayne can opener, from his Marine Corps days, out of his *parfleche.* "Yum, goes good with a cold camp...Sure would like some coffee, though."

"Me too, but we're too close to have a fire...Want to suck on some ground Arbuckles'?"

"Pass."

The morning sun glinted red off the scattered clouds as it peeked above the eastern horizon. The gold, orange, red, and yellow leaves along with an occasional splash of green from cedar and pine trees created a cacophony of color over the hills.

Wiley sat up on his blanket and looked at the sky. "Uhhh, don't like that."

Harper tried to look up, but his throat was too sore. He had tied his wild rag around it to keep the cut clean.

"What's the matter?"

"My daddy was a seaman. Used to say, 'Red sky at night...sailor's delight. Red sky at mornin'...sailor take warnin'...Jesus even says it in the Bible."

"Yer funnin' me."

"Nope, my mama said it's in the book of Matthew som'ers...She read the Bible ever night."

"That means a storm comin'?"

Wiley nodded. "What they say."

Carson set up and rubbed his eyes. "Ezzard made the coffee yet?"

The others looked around.

Slim got to his feet and stepped over to Ezzard's empty blanket. "Ezzard's gone, Boss...an' so's the poke sack with the coffee an' bacon in it."

Carson shot to his feet. "The hell?"

Slim nodded. "Yep, he's gone, shore...but all his stuff's still here."

Lou looked at the woods. "Meby he's takin' a leak."

Carson shook his head. "He'd of put the coffee on first."

"But like I said, Boss...Coffee was in the poke sack. It's gone."

Carson turned with fury in his eyes and stepped over to Ames. "You little worm, you were 'sposed to be on guard."

"I wuz on guard, nobody come in er out."

Carson shoved the smaller man to the ground. "Don't lie to me."

Lou jumped up. "Hey...Boss er no boss, you can't pick on him."

Carson turned to Lou. "Thought you two didn't like each other...fightin' all the time."

"Done that all our lives. He's my little brother. Anybody gonna shove him...it'll be me."

"Don't need no help, Brother. I kin tend to his hash by myself...Ain't nobody gonna call me a liar."

He pitched his rifle to Lou and stepped toward Carson with his fists up in front of his face.

Carson showed his palms to Ames. "Awright, sorry. Maybe I jumped to conclusions."

"Yeah, I'd say." Ames didn't put his fists down.

Carson turned to the others. "'Nybody see Ezzard when that fire flared up?"

Slim nodded. "He was there when I come down from the cave...wuz asleep when somebody throwed more logs on the fire."

"Did 'nybody see who added the logs?"

They all exchanged glances and shook their heads.

Carson looked around. "We'll get the hell outta here in the mornin' after Coltrane shows us where that box is...Slim, add some water to the grounds in the pot. Know it'll be weak, but beats nothin'...I ain't 'bout to get back in the sack."

There were several, 'Me neithers.'

They all heard the same eerie laughter they'd heard earlier. As before, everyone drew their sidearms to fire in the direction it sounded like it was coming from.

"What the..."

Harper was the first to pull his trigger—the hammer clicked. He flipped the gate open as each of the others tried to shoot, also.

"Empty." He looked around without turning his head.

Slim nodded. "Mine, too."

Carson checked his. "An' mine."

Lou, Ames, and Wiley all concurred, theirs weren't loaded either.

Everyone immediately reloaded their pieces and looked nervously around at the early morning shadows in the forest. None of them could have seen anything because their eyes couldn't adjust quickly enough.

Bone turned to Loraine. "Dang, I'm good."

"Shame they don't realize they could have all been dead as well."

Bone nodded. "Want to put the fear of God in 'em first. No need in killin' 'em if I can scare 'em half to death...More fun this way." He giggled.

§§§

CHAPTER NINETEEN

SEVEN DEVILS

"Mister Ira, there's something wrong with my daddy."

Ira stepped inside the cave. "What is it, girly?" He squinted his eyes in the partial darkness.

"I don't know. I shook his shoulder an' he's not moving...Somethin's wrong."

Ira propped his rifle against the wall of the old mine, leaned over Coltrane and put his hand on his shoulder.

Alice popped him on the back of the head with a rock. It wasn't hard enough to knock him out, but was enough to drop him to his knees and grab his head.

"Ow, ow!"

Jip snatched the pistol from Ira's holster and stuck it under his chin. "Now, Slick, I want to know who hired you boys...Don't aim to ask twice."

"Dang it, you did have a knife. Son-of-a-gun"

Coltrane poked his chin a little harder with the muzzle and glared at him with his steel-gray eyes.

"Awright, awright." Ira took a breath and rubbed the back of his head. "Don't know the guy's name, Carson set up the meet. Just know he was some high-dollar guy, 'bout fifty, er so...Dressed fancy an' had a bit of a paunch on 'im...Met him in Paris. All I know, swear to God."

"Uh-huh." Jip thought a moment, then hit Ira with a devastating left uppercut to the jaw. The man collapsed to the floor of the cave like a pile of dirty laundry and didn't move.

"He'll be out for a while. Should be able to get around the camp an' head to where I've got Red picketed."

"Know who he was talking about, Daddy?"

He pursed his lips. "Maybe."

Coltrane turned his head at the sound of distant thunder rolling across the morning skies to the northwest.

"Jump on my back an' we'll head down the hill."

Harper nudged Lou and nodded toward the trail over to where the horses were. He turned to Carson.

"We're done here, Carson. Ya'll can have whatever money you can get Coltrane to show you."

Harper's men turned toward the trail.

"Hell you say."

Harper, Lou, and Ames turned back to look down the barrels of three pistols in the hands of Carson, Slim, and Wiley as each of them thumbed the hammers back.

"Nobody walks out on me."

The banty rooster, Ames, stepped forward and got in Carson's face. "We had 'nough of this crazy place, Jaybird. We're gone." He started to turn and Carson pulled the trigger, shooting the little man in the side.

Ames fell to the ground writhing in pain, holding his side.

Lou went for his Colt, but the three turned their .45s on him. He changed his mind, bent over and picked his brother up in his arms with tears in his eyes.

"We're goin' home." Lou turned and headed down the trail toward the horses.

Harper, hands at his side, backed to the trail, turned and followed the brothers.

Slim looked at Carson. "Now what?"

"Less ways to split, that's what." He holstered his Remington. "Let's go up an' get the lawdog."

Bone glanced at Loraine. "Figured something like this would happen. Let's go back, get the horses an' bring 'em up closer...Think this is about to come to a head."

She nodded. "Think so."

A long rolling peal of thunder rumbled across the sky. "We may get wet."

Bone looked up at the dark clouds headed their way and shrugged. "Could happen...Sounds like God opened his bowlin' alley...Come on, Big Guy."

He, Loraine, and Bear Dog headed the mile back to where they left Hildebrandt and Sweet Face.

Coltrane and Alice squatted down in the bushes at the report of the pistol from the camp.

"What happened, Daddy?"

"Sounds like there is a bit of a disagreement amongst the brigands, Honey...an' that's a good thing. Come on...better hurry."

Alice straddled his back once again, wrapping her legs about his waist and her arms around his neck.

They arched around the camp back to the tree where he'd stashed his knife, gun, and gunbelt.

Coltrane set her down, brushed the leaves away at the base of the tree, removed the wild rag from his Colt, and blew what little dirt had gotten inside away before checking the chambers and buckling the gunbelt back around his hips.

"You had this all planned, didn't you?"

He smiled. "Pretty much. Wasn't quite sure how it was goin' to shake out, but wanted to be ready."

They jumped at the sharp sound of lightning striking on the other side of the ridge. The black clouds overhead were churning and rolling.

"How close was that?"

"Sounded like it was just the other side of that ridge, probably a little less than a mile. Lightnin' can fool you sometimes an' sound closer than it is."

Carson, Wiley, and Slim worked their way up to the cave.

"Where the hell's Ira?" Carson looked at Slim.

"Don't know...Ira? Where are you?"

They heard a groan from the cave and went inside. Ira sat up and felt his jaw.

"What in hell happened?"

"Sucker punched me, Carson. Did have a knife. Don't know where it was, but damn shore had one."

Slim held up Ira's Winchester. "Didn't take yer rifle."

Ira felt around. "Got my Colt, though. Reckon didn't want to tote that rifle 'long with that gal."

Wiley looked at him. "Wha'd'a mean?"

Carson frowned. "Why do you think we took her shoes, Stupid. He's carryin' her, shore...Come on, caint' have gotten far. Slim, yer a fair-to-middlin' tracker...see as you can find which way they went."

He nodded. "Should be easy 'nuff...carryin' her."

They stepped outside and he found their tracks at the same time lightning struck the other side of the ridge.

Wiley jerked. "Damnation, hate lightnin'."

The thunder rolled.

The dead pine tree the bolt of lightning struck less than a half-mile away showered sparks down to the ground on top of the newly fallen leaves—smoke began to curl up, spread right and left and inched toward the top of the ridge with ever-gaining speed.

Bone lifted his head. "Smoke. Ground fire somewhere." He held up a wet finger. "That way, north, other side of the ridge."

Bone turned and headed toward the area they left the horses.

"Shouldn't we try to find Coltrane and his daughter, first?"

"Nope, got a better idea."

Loraine pointed toward the visible smoke curling over the top of the ridge. "But that fire."

"The Indians periodically set fires this time of year to burn the fallen leaves. Helps the winter grass and kills most of the underbrush...Sap's still movin' in the trees, so they're not gonna burn. Pretty smart, you ask me. Good stewards of the land...an' helps the huntin'."

"Hope you know what you're doing."

"When have you ever...no, never mind, don't answer that."

Slim led Carson, Wiley, and Ira down the ridge and picked up Coltrane's tracks in a game trail. The men increased their pace to a jog.

They rounded the camp and headed south.

"There!" Slim spotted Coltrane with his daughter on his back as they rounded a bend in the trail.

The men drew their pistols and commenced firing at the pair.

Coltrane quickly set Alice down. "Stay in the trail, Honey, you should be all right...Go."

"But, Daddy..."

"Do it...Go." He turned and fired at the oncoming four men.

They returned it. Bullets whipped through the lower hanging branches and colorful fall leaves, sending many that hadn't yet fallen drifting to the ground.

Bone's head snapped back. "Gun fight! Just like my vision. Come on, Babe, gotta hurry."

Bear Dog moved out in front of them at a lope as they neared the creek where the horses were picketed.

They splashed through the wide, but shallow, clear stream to the glade where the horses were grazing.

Hildebrandt was the first to look up as Bear Dog waded out of the water and shook. He nickered.

More gunfire echoed through the valley...

§§§

CHAPTER TWENTY

SEVEN DEVILS

Carson's men chased Coltrane and his daughter down the narrow game trail, occasionally firing at them.

Ira carried his rifle. He raised it, pointed toward the running pair, and fired—missed. It's very difficult to fire a weapon, especially a rifle, as you run—much more so than from horseback.

Tendrils of smoke from the rapidly advancing wall of fire coming down the ridge were wafting through the trees. The flames were spreading to the right and to the left as they raced downhill.

Bone and Loraine splashed through the thigh-deep water and up on the bank. He approached Hildebrandt easily so he wouldn't spook him and completely undid the loose cinch as well as the rear girth and pulled his saddle and blanket from his back.

"What are you doing?"

"Taking his tack off. Ground fire shouldn't cross this creek without wind...a tree fire, maybe yes."

Loraine shook her head and frowned, still not understanding what he was doing as he also pulled the bridle from Hildebrandt's head.

"What about Sweet Face?"

"No need."

She frowned again.

The burning wall of fire raced on downhill, consuming the dead leaves like a voracious dragon. The flames were moving at better than ten miles per hour, with each end of the wall curling around as they sought the most leaves to burn. Smoke was being carried above the treetops in swirling columns.

Forest critters and birds fled the fire, escaping downhill toward streams and creeks. Most were well on their way even as the fire burned on the other side of the ridge—their survival sense of impending danger took over.

Coltrane kept his body between the men behind them and Alice—just in case.

He emptied Ira's Colt and pitched it into the brush at the side of the trail and drew his own ivory-gripped Colt Single Action Army .45.

Jip turned his upper body and snapped off two quick rounds from the more familiar handgun.

Carson and his men were a little less than a hundred feet behind them—Slim, in the lead, caught one of the rounds in the center of his chest and collapsed, to his back, in the middle of the trail.

Carson, directly behind Slim, stumbled over him as he fell. Wiley and Ira had time to either jump over the two men or step around them as Carson was trying to get up.

Ira momentarily stopped, now that he had a more clear shot, and cranked off a round at Coltrane from his Winchester.

The lawman stumbled and fell to his knees in the trail. Alice turned her head, saw her father go down, screamed, turned around, and ran back to him.

He pushed her away. "No! Go, go, go...this trail will lead to where Red is. Go, now!"

She grabbed the sides of her full skirt, and resumed running down the trail.

Coltrane, still on his knees, turned, took careful aim using a two-handed grip, and dropped Ira with one shot.

Carson and Wiley, seeing they were down to just them, took cover behind some trees at the side of the trail.

Coltrane did the same, knowing he could stop them from catching Alice as long as the ammo in his gunbelt held out. He looked up at the thickening smoke in the trees.

"Uh-oh." He ripped the sleeve from his shirt and tied it around his bleeding calf. "Didn't hit the artery, thank goodness."

Jip peeked out around the tree he was behind back up the trail and up at the side of the ridge. The glow from the wall of flames was plainly visible through the trees behind Carson and Wiley.

He got to his feet, limped through the trees, and rejoined the trail forty feet further down. Coltrane found a hickory limb and used it like a cane to help him limp along.

Alice turned around, disobeying her father, and headed back to help him.

They almost ran into each other.

"What was it about 'No, go, go, go', you didn't understand?"

"You're hurt. I wasn't about to leave you...like you wouldn't leave me...End of the discussion."

She put his left arm around her shoulders as he used the stick to help on the right—they made much better time as the smoke continued to thicken.

Bone motioned to Bear Dog as he stood beside Hildebrandt. He pointed toward the ridge.

"Find, boys...Find."

Bear Dog and Hildebrandt immediately turned, almost as one, and splashed across the stream like they could read Bone's mind—maybe they could. They disappeared from view in the trees in seconds.

Loraine turned to Bone with her eyes wide. "They're runnin' straight toward the fire!"

He nodded. "I know."

Wiley glanced over at Carson behind another tree. "Think he's gone."

Carson looked around at the gathering smoke. "We'd best be gone, too. Let's git back to the horses."

They joined up back on the trail and headed toward the small glade where the horses were picketed as fast as they could.

The closer they got to the small glen, the thicker the smoke became.

Wiley pointed at some movement in the trees up ahead. "Damnation, Carson...there go the horses!"

They could just make out at least six up ahead running as fast as they could through the trees in the smoky haze.

"Yeah, they busted loose an' 're headed to safety...away from that fire. We'd better do the same."

Wiley turned and followed Carson in the same direction the horses were running. "Reckon we kin outrun it?"

"Better."

The two outlaws picked up their pace.

Bear Dog led the way through the trees with Hildebrandt on his heels. The smoke continued to get thicker the farther they ran.

The wolf-dog led them between two arms of the flames. There was a wall of fire on both sides of them, now, but the gallant pair didn't slow down.

They burst through the trees into one of the numerous game trails that ran throughout the Seven Devil hills.

"Look, Daddy!"

Alice pointed just ahead of them in the trail. Bear Dog stood in the middle and *woofed* at them while Hildebrandt reared up on his back legs with a loud whinny.

The massive horse danced around in front of Coltrane and Alice as they hobbled up to them.

"Try to get on him, Honey. Get out of here. No way I can climb on...Now go, please!" He turned to hug her.

"Oh, Daddy, what's he doing?"

Alice pointed at Hildebrandt.

"Oh, my God...He knows. He's kneeling down."

Hildebrandt knelt on his front knees with his head down.

"He wants us to get on."

"Looks like it. Go ahead."

"No, you get on first, I'll get behind you."

"Dang, girl, you're hardheaded like your mama."

Coltrane leaned across Hildebrandt's whithers since he couldn't put weight on his left leg. He swung both legs around and straddled the big animal.

HILDEBRANDT & BEAR DOG

Alice quickly mounted behind him, extended her arms around his waist and entwined her hands in Hildebrandt's long black mane.

Coltrane had his hands twisted in the mane a little further up his neck.

Hildebrant gathered first one leg, then the other and stood back up.

Bear Dog *woofed* again, spun around and darted through the swirling smoke back down the trial they way they'd come.

Hildebrandt charged right behind him directly at a wall of flames.

Alice leaned forward on Coltrane's back. "Daddy! We're surrounded! There's fire all around us!"

§§§

CHAPTER TWENTY-ONE

SEVEN DEVILS

"Lay down on the ground, Babe, less smoke there."

"Not much." Loraine squinted her eyes to try to see across the creek into the denser smoke of the woods. "Where are they?"

"They'll be here, soon...I hope."

"Love your confidence."

"They're comin'...I still feel 'em."

"I think that's my leg."

"Oh, right."

"How do you know they'll find Coltrane and Alice?"

He shrugged. "Well, there was, or I guess there will be, a horse the Marines use in the Korean war known as *Reckless*. She was primarily used to transport ammo across the battlefield. Someone figured they'd see if she would carry wounded Marines off the field back to the doctors."

"During the battle?"

"Right...well, she made fifty-seven trips with the wounded...all unaided by a trainer. They'd tie one or two men to her back and she'd carry them to the field hospital, then go back for more...all under fire. She received eleven medals and commendations, including two purple hearts, plus an official promotion to the rank of Staff Sergeant...There's a statue of her in our time at the National Museum of the Marine Corps in Quantico, Virginia."

"Oh, my goodness."

"So, I know Hildebrandt and Bear Dog can and will do it."

"There's fire everywhere!"

"I know, Honey. Keep your head down on top of me." Coltrane laid as close to Hildebrandt's neck as he could.

Burning leaves swirled about in small eddies similar to dust devils as the wall of fire moved downslope. Sparks danced just above the ground from the air movement created by the heat of the blazing fire.

"Can't see anything but fire, Daddy, can you?"

"No, Honey. Just have to trust in the Lord and these angels he sent...Try to hold your breath."

"Trying."

Bear Dog unerringly picked the thinnest sections of the burning wall to go through—Hildebrandt faithfully followed where he led.

Bone and Loraine never took their eyes off the line of woods across the creek, even as the leaves on the forest floor under them caught fire.

"Bone!"

He saw what Loraine saw at the same moment.

Bear Dog burst through the wall of fire at the edge of the creek and Hildebrandt scattered burning leaves into the air as he came through right behind him. They hit the creek at almost the same time, splashing across the forty-foot waterway together.

Hildebrandt lunged up on the bank in front of Bone and Loraine and stopped—his sides heaving as his muscles quivered.

Bone and Loraine jumped up and pulled the near-unconscious Alice and Coltrane from Hildebrandt's back.

The bottom of the big horse's long, thick, tail still smoldered. The ends of the tail hair had caught fire but were extinguished when they crossed the creek.

Bear Dog's hair also showed signs of being singed.

Once Coltrane and Alice were off his back, Hildebrandt joined Bear Dog back at the creek drinking their fill of the cool water.

Alice looked up from the ground as Loraine patted a couple of places on the ends of her long blonde hair to make sure they weren't more than singed.

"Who are ya'll?" She looked over at her father. "Daddy?"

"I'm all right, Honey." He looked down as Bone tended to his wounded leg. "Like she asked, who are ya'll?"

"They call me Bone an' that's my wife, Loraine."

He cleaned up the dried blood from Coltrane's bullet wound after ripping his pant leg up to the knee to get to it.

"You're lucky...Well, don't guess gettin' shot is ever lucky, but in your case, it's what we call a through-an'-through. Not gonna have to dig anything out." He handed him a small piece of latigo. Here, bite down on this, I'm fixin' to sew the holes up...probably smart some."

Bone stuck the leather strip in Coltrane's mouth, rinsed the holes with whiskey from a flask he carried in his saddlebags, and started stitching the two wounds up.

Sweat broke out on Jip's face as Bone pulled the black linen thread through his skin and tied each one off with a surgical knot.

"Well, that wasn't too bad, only took four sutures each." He poured a little more whiskey over each wound.

"Ay-yi-yi...Easy for you to say...Now 'bout the question."

"Oh, that...Mason sent us. We're cops from...well, let's say from Gainesville."

"Ah, Bone. Right, heard him mention you."

"Wasn't me, I wasn't there, an' I didn't do it."

"From what he said, you probably did."

"Can you get word to my mama, Mister Bone?"

He glanced at Alice, then back to Coltrane as thunder rolled again.

They looked up at the heavy black clouds hanging low overhead as the first few king-sized drops began to fall.

Loraine helped Alice to her feet, then stepped over to her and Bone's saddles. She removed their ponchos tied behind the cantles and took them over to where Bone and Coltrane were.

Alice helped her and Bone spread the large rain covers over their heads as the next rumble of thunder shook the rain lose from the laden clouds.

The drops fell in sheets, drenching everything around, including the remaining leaves feeding the ground fire—the last of the flames were soon extinguished.

HILDEBRANDT & BEAR DOG

Hildebrandt stood with his head lowered and his ears flat to keep the rain from getting inside them.

Bear Dog sat on his haunches underneath his big friend.

Loraine glanced out from under the poncho. "Bear Dog, Hildebrandt, Sweet Face, and your horse, Jip, seem to be enjoying the rain."

"Do, don't they?...His name is Red."

Bone nodded. "Fits."

"Actually, bought him from Mason when I took over the sheriff's office for Jack County when he retired and moved to Cooke County."

Loraine smiled. "Thought he looked familiar. He's been here in the Seven Devils before...when Mason and Fiona were with us, Texas Ranger Bodie Hickman, and Marshal Bass Reeves when we were protecting Theodore Roosevelt."

Coltrane nodded. "Always wanted to meet the great Bass Reeves...He's a real American hero."

Bone chuckled. "He's everything they say...plus some."

"Mister Bone, can we get word to my mama?...She's all right, isn't she?"

Bone glanced up. "Looks like the rain's slackin' off."

"Mister Bone?"

He finally looked at Alice, then at Loraine. No words were necessary between them.

Loraine put her arm around Alice's shoulders. "Honey...this isn't easy to say..."

Alice looked at Loraine, then at her father. "What is it? What's wrong?"

Loraine took a breath. "Alice, your mother's gone...they found her hanging from a rafter in your barn...It was made to look like she committed suicide because you had been kidnapped...I'm so sorry."

"No! No!"

Alice buried her face in Loraine's bosom—the tears flowed as her shoulders shook.

The teenager's lithe body shook with sobs as she tried to take a breath.

Carson and Wiley, soaked to the skin, worked their way in the direction the horses had run.

"Now that the rain put the fire out, the horses will stop soon...We'll find 'em."

Wiley glanced at Carson. "Dang shore hope so. Got no desire to walk all the way to Lukfala."

The stench of wet, burned leaves was almost overpowering.

"Me neither. That stink from them burnt leaves is 'bout to gag me."

"Well, leastwise most of it's behind us an' the rain come 'fore we wuz caught in the fire."

Carson nodded. "Yeah, there's that."

They clambered down a deer-cut in the side of a wide, ten-foot deep gully. Carson and Wiley followed the tracks of the horses as they ran along the bottom.

The ravine made a blind turn to the south.

Wiley stopped in front of Carson and staggered back, bumping into him. "Oh, sweet Mary, Mother of God!"

"What?" Carson looked around Wiley. "Oh, Jesus." He bent over and threw up at the side of the trail.

Ezzard and Williams sat back-to-back in the middle of the trail. Their heads were tied together with a strip of leather—with their throats slashed to the bone. Blood covered the fronts of both men. Their faces had Shamanistic symbols painted on them in red ocher.

Wiley slowly approached the bodies and looked closely at them, then back at Carson as the man was wiping his mouth on his sleeve.

"Carson, ain't them like old Injun symbols?"

"Yeah. Looks like it...Don't think they want us here."

Wiley turned back to Carson after looking at the ancient Indian drawings. "Uh...they clothes ain't wet."

"What're you sayin'?"

A pale Wiley shook his head. "Just that. They wadn't here when it rained just a little bit ago..."

Bone and Loraine shook their ponchos to remove any water remaining before rolling them back up.

A red-eyed Alice still sat in an almost catatonic state on the ground, staring off in the distance. Bear Dog laid beside her with his head on her knee trying to comfort her.

Bone put his hand on Coltrane's shoulder. "Like I mentioned. Jip, someone tried to make it look like she committed suicide, but Loraine and I determined from seeing the photos the coroner took, that it was murder...Some folks in Jacksboro even think you might have done it since you disappeared."

Coltrane nodded and pursed his lips. "Somebody sure wanted me to come here and I'm pretty sure I know why."

"That box we heard them mention?"

He nodded, then took a breath and shook his head. "They think it's full of gold, but what they don't know…"

"Bone! Listen." Loraine pointed back in the direction of the camp.

He glanced at Coltrane. "Men…screaming."

§§§

CHAPTER TWENTY-TWO

SEVEN DEVILS

Bone peered through the occasional tendrils of residual smoke from the leaves drifting up on the other side of the creek.

"I'd say all the fires are out over there."

Coltrane glanced at Alice. "Baby, do you want to go with us back to the camp? Thought we'd see if they left anything...like maybe your shoes?"

She shook her head. "Uh-uh, Daddy, ya'll go ahead. Think I'll wait here, if you don't mind."

"That's fine, Honey."

"I'll stay with her. Ya'll don't need me. I'll put on some coffee an' something on to eat." Loraine looked at Alice. "Are you hungry, Alice?"

"Not really, Miz Bone, but you can fix something for ya'll."

"It's Loraine, Honey." She winked at Coltrane.

He nodded. "We'll be back in just a bit." Jip turned to Bone. "Walk or ride?"

"Well, I'd say walk." He glanced over at Hildebrandt. "Think he's done his duty for today...Let him rest a bit. It's a little less than a mile, I figure."

"I would say so." He stepped over and kissed Alice on her forehead and turned back to Bone.

HILDEBRANDT & BEAR DOG

"Ready?"

"Let's go."

Bear Dog jumped up and headed for the creek.

"You don't have to go either, Big Guy."

He turned, looked at Bone, cocked his head and gave him his smile.

"So, it's going to be that way is it?"

Bear Dog woofed, splashed into the creek, and swam to the other side. He shook as he waited on Bone and Coltrane to cross.

"You sure he can't talk?"

"Oh, he can, it's just a different language than we use."

Coltrane smiled and nodded. "Yeah, but he's pretty easy to understand."

"Noticed that, did you?"

"Could say."

The two large men waded through the thigh-deep water. Coltrane was only about four inches shorter than Bone's 6'8" and around forty pounds lighter than Bone's 285—still a big man for the time.

They worked their way toward the camp through the damp, burnt leaves.

"Stink, don't they?" Coltrane looked at Bone.

"Yeah, lot better'n burnt meat, though."

"Good point."

They entered the empty camp.

"Looks like they all got out, but their stuff is still here. I'll see if I can find Alice's shoes."

Bone nodded. "I'll go over and check where their horses were. Back in a jif."

"Jif?"

"Uh...jiffy. You know, quick-like."

"Oh, right. Just not a word I've heard often."

"Yeah. We use it...uh, back home a lot."

"Uh-huh."

Bone and Bear Dog headed down the trail to the glade where the horses were kept.

He looked around at the torn-up ground and the broken ropes and picket pins jerked out of the ground. Bear Dog sniffed at the torn-up sod and looked back at Bone.

"Uh-huh, horse wants to leave...they'll leave. Got out of Dodge while they had the chance, looks like." Bone looked at three of the ropes. "Yep, three of 'em came and got their horses...What'dya got, Boy?" He ran his fingers on a stain on some of the grass that Bear Dog was standing over. "Somebody was wounded...Bet a nickel it was the three from the train. Didn't think they fit with that bunch anyway."

The wolf-dog *woofed*.

He looked around again to make sure he didn't miss anything and headed back to the camp.

Bone walked in and Coltrane was holding a black pair of ladies button-up shoes.

"See you found 'em."

"Good thing. Don't think I could carry her again...what with this leg."

"How is it, by the way?"

"Sore as a risin', but could be worse."

Bone nodded. "Could that...Ready to head back?"

"Guess so. Horses gone?"

"Yeah, all but three either broke their tethers or jerked the picket pins up. The other three had been untied...So, I make it three of our friends left before the fire started."

"The three new guys?"

"My thoughts...One of 'em was wounded."

"Alice an' I heard a single shot after we left the cave...figured they weren't gettin' along."

"Suspect they're long gone."

"Most likely."

"Think we should see where that screamin' came from?"

Coltrane nodded. "Do...Sounded to me like it came from that way." He pointed off to the east.

"That's the direction the horses went after they busted loose."

HILDEBRANDT & BEAR DOG

Bone and Coltrane headed off to the east and intersected the tracks of running horses. Bear Dog loped ahead, nose to the ground.

"They were in a panic...tryin' to get away from the fire." Bone pointed at the hoof prints.

"Seems like there's a shallow draw that way, animals use it regular."

"You're familiar with it, I take it."

"Lived near here when I was a kid...That draw's right up there."

They followed the tracks down the deer-cut to the bottom and followed the draw south.

Bear Dog stopped in his tracks, the hair along his back rose up.

"Holy Mother of God!"

Coltrane and Bone stopped right behind him when they rounded a sharp bend. There in the trail were the bodies of Carson, Wiley, Williams, and Ezzard, all back-to-back with their heads bound together, like a big four leaf clover. Each man's throat was slashed and their faces painted in Indian symbols with red ocher.

Bear Dog circled the four men, not getting too close. His hackles were still up.

"Lordy, Lordy, slap Aunt Gussie in the face...looks like they got caught in their own loop."

"The Choctaws say they're's evil spirits in these hills...certain types of people don't do well here...Say they got the stories from the Caddo."

"Never argue with old Indian legends." Bone looked at Coltrane. "What say we light a shuck ourselves?"

"Best idea I've heard."

They turned and headed back toward the creek and Bone's camp.

Bear Dog looked back once more at the bodies, then turned and caught up with Bone and Coltrane.

"Think you know who was behind all this...that hired those jacklegs?"

"Uh-huh, got a fair idea...A distant cousin of mine...third step-cousin or somethin' like that. Always been jealous of the money the Coltranes had...mines, land, cattle an' so on."

"Yep, common enough."

"You mentioned you didn't think my wife committed suicide?"

Bone nodded. "Yeah, it's the cop in me. My bride an' I saw the pictures the Jack County Coroner took...that's a good practice, by the way."

"I would think so."

"Anyway...an' you'll forgive me for gettin' graphic...she was hanging from a rafter with her feet about two feet above the floor of the barn."

Coltrane pursed his lips. "And?"

"And, there was nothing close for her to have stood on in order to put the noose around her neck. No box, stool, chair...nothin'. Kinda hard to do."

"She was fine when I left to go after the men who took Alice...Upset, of course, but certainly not at herself...No way she'd of done herself harm."

"Understandable."

"The person behind all this wanted me to chase after the men that took our daughter. Don't think they expected me to find them quite so soon."

"And then whoever it was, killed your wife to make a point they meant business...wouldn't hesitate to kill Alice, either, if they didn't get what they wanted."

"Exactly."

They exited the woods at the creek and waded across.

Bear Dog splashed across first and ran up to the newcomers.

"Well, look what the cat drug in...Mason, what are you an' Fiona doin' here?"

Mason stepped forward after setting his coffee cup on the ground. "That's the thanks we get. Came thinkin' ya'll might need some help, 'specially seein' the smoke from the forest fire before the rain...Shoulda known better."

"Everything worked in our favor...includin' the spirits."

Fiona looked at Bone. "Spirits? As in ghosts?"

"Whatever you want to call 'em, Fiona...they were certainly out an' about. Mostly playin' havoc with the bad guys."

"Jip, you look none the worse for wear, except for your leg there."

"Thanks to Bone's horse and that wolf-dog there. We were in a world of hurt till they found us...the fire was almost on us an' I was shot in the leg."

Coltrane looked at Bone. "Speakin' of, probably ought to change the dressin' on this thing since it got wet in the creek...twice."

Bone nodded. "Sit down...Fiona, don't suppose you got some of Angie's miracle salve, do you?"

Fiona smiled. "Just so happens." She walked over to her painted mule, Spot, and removed a small jar from her saddlebags. "Here. Just what the doctor ordered." She pitched it to Bone.

Coltrane glanced at the jar. "What's that?"

Bone unscrewed the lid and sniffed the contents. "Oh, some stuff Marshal McGann's wife, Angie, makes. They live over in the Arbuckles...Old Irish concoction."

"Of?"

"She won't say everything that's in it, but it's mostly hog tallow an' turpentine. Jack says it'll heal up an' hair over a cat's butt in three days."

"Bone!"

He turned to Loraine. "Well, he does."

"We have minors present, you know."

Alice grinned. "I know what a cat's butt is, Loraine."

"Anyway, this stuff is a-mazing."

Bone stepped over, pushed Coltrane's torn pant leg up above his boot top, and cut the bandage loose with his pocket knife. He held out his hand to Loraine.

"Whiskey."

She handed him the flask. He poured some of the one hundred proof alcohol on both sets of stitches.

"Ooo, ow, ow...Gollybum."

"Don't be such a baby, Daddy."

"I'll baby you, Little Girl."

Bone smeared a dab of the salve on both wounds and nodded to Loraine to wrap it up with the bandages she already had in her hand.

Flynn nodded. "Good job, Bone." He turned to Coltrane. "Now for the bad news."

"Uh-oh, now what?"

Mason pulled a folded document from his pocket. "Got a warrant for your arrest, Jip, for the..." He looked at Alice. "I'm sorry, Honey,"

She nodded. "Go ahead, Uncle Flynn, I've pretty well gotten immune to almost anything."

He turned back to Coltrane. "A warrant for the murder of Alicia Coltrane...your wife."

Alice's hand went to her mouth as she gasped.

"Issued by?"

"Jack County Judge Leonard Keeler."

Coltrane looked at Bone and nodded. "That third step-cousin I mentioned."

§§§

CHAPTER TWENTY-THREE

SEVEN DEVILS

"Does the coroner know when..." Coltrane took a breath. "...when Alicia died?"

Mason nodded. "Your deputy, Harlan Platt, went by your house when you didn't show up at the office at nine as usual. He found her when he looked for you in the barn."

"When did the coroner check the body, Mason?"

"Right away, Bone. First thing Platt did was to go get him."

"Any idea what state of rigor she was in?"

"Interesting you should ask...she was in full rigor when the coroner got out there around ten."

Coltrane looked at Bone. "What does that have to do with it?"

"Everything...depending on when you left town after the men that took Alice."

He frowned. "Meaning?"

"Onset of rigor mortis is within four hours of death and normally lasts no more than eight hours at normal ambient temperature. At the time of morning, when she died, the temperature would be around seventy-five degrees."

Coltrane turned to Mason. "Platt then came out to our place on the morning of the nineteenth, correct?"

"That's what the report says, why?"

"I left town around four PM the previous day...soon as I discovered Alice was missing. I found the tracks of six horses, as well as signs of a struggle..."

"I fought 'em, Daddy, hard as I could. It was that Carson man, the one called Slim, an' three others. Man called Curtis, another named Wiley, an' a third man, Ezzard....They had a spare horse for me. They gagged me and put me on him...Those last three left our camp early the next day before daylight. Don't know where they went."

Bone nodded. "Think I do."

Coltrane looked at Alice. "That's what I figured, Baby, from the signs. I told Alicia, immediately got my gear, saddled Red, an' lit out."

"You happen to stop in town or anywhere that someone might have seen you?"

He turned to Bone again. "Did...Stopped at Sewell's Mercantile to get an extra box of cartridges an' a couple pounds of Arbuckles', why?"

"Well, if Alicia was in full rigor..."

"Oh, I see. She was murdered early the morning of the nineteenth an' I'd been gone over fifteen hours...Those other three men."

Loraine nodded. "Bingo, there's no way you could have even known."

Coltrane turned to Loraine. "What's 'bingo'?"

She looked at Bone. "He doesn't know, does he?"

"Uh-uh." He shook his head.

"Just as well tell them, make things a lot easier."

"Tell us what?" Alice looked at both Loraine and Bone.

Bone nodded and turned to Coltrane and Alice. She was sitting on the log beside him.

"Uh...Loraine an' I are not from this time, ya'll."

Alice frowned and glanced at her dad, then back to Bone. "What are you saying?"

Bone's eyebrows went up with an almost sheepish look. "Well, see, we're actually from the year 2018...We were accidentally transported here in 1898 through an ancient Indian portal in Palo Pinto County during a lightning storm."

He put his arm around Loraine's shoulders. "We were going fishing at a big lake they built in our time on the Brazos called Possum Kingdom Lake."

She elbowed him in the ribs. "I had never been fishing before so, for some reason he picked that lake...This huge storm came up an' we had to take refuge in an old cave. There were all sorts of Indian petroglyphs on the walls, including this spiral thing..."

Bone nodded. "Uh-huh...an' those spirals are seen all over the world. Many archeologists believe they're symbols for inter-dimensional, or time portals..."

"Lightning hit the hill where the cave was an' when we came out...the lake was gone."

He squeezed her shoulders. "My baby asked me, 'Where are we?', on account the lake wasn't there anymore, but I recognized the hills around, knew they were the same an' could tell the river down below was the Brazos. I looked at her an' said, 'No, Pard, not where are we?...When are we?'...eventually figured out it was 1898."

Loraine smiled and shrugged. "Been here ever since...We were partners at the Gainesville Police Department. Bone was a Homicide Detective and I was an Inspector...We finally figured out we were in love and got married three years ago."

Coltrane smiled. "That's why ya'll know so much about criminal investigations an' such...Wondered about those weapons ya'll carry...Never seen anything like 'em."

Alice beamed. "It's like Mark Twain's, *A Connecticut Yankee in King Author's*

Court...or H. G. Wells', *The Time Machine.*"

Bone shrugged. "Well, close enough, Alice, except those are fiction...We're for real." He held out his arm. "Pinch."

Loraine backhanded him across the chest.

Fiona looked at Alice and Jip. "Now ya'll know so we don't have to dance on egg shells any more."

Bone glanced at Fiona. "Except for the part about finding out that Fiona and Mason are actually my great grandparents."

Alice's jaw dropped open. "Whaaat?"

Fiona nodded. "True. Bone took a bullet meant for me and saved my life...had he not, he would have never existed...But if he ever calls me 'Grandma', I'll shoot him myself."

Alice looked puzzled. "I don't understand."

Bone grinned. "Yeah, gives me a headache thinkin' about it sometimes, too, Hon. We'll have a friend, Chickasaw

Shaman *Anompoli Lawa,* explain it to you when we get back to Gainesville."

Coltrane chuckled and shook his head. "Yeah, noticed Bone being a bit evasive about some things."

Mason glanced at Fiona. "Only problem is, ya'll, we still have to jump through the legal hoops. The warrant has been issued." He turned to Coltrane. "Got to take you in, Jip...sorry. The law is the law."

"I understand, Mason...Would do the same."

"Loraine an' I will testify...and with the help of the coroner's report, there's no doubt we can prove you weren't even in town when she was murdered."

"Well, I'll have to depend on ya'll...I can only tell the truth. The jury will believe me or not."

Bone glanced at Loraine then back to Coltrane. "Can't argue with facts."

Loraine nodded. "Unless you're a Democrat...By the way, what was all that about a copper box with gold or money in it?"

Coltrane chuckled. "Tell ya'll what...how 'bout I just show it to you?"

Bone shrugged. "Why not, we're here."

"It's over near that outlaw camp...Walk or ride?"

Bone got to his feet. "Ride. Done enough walkin' for a bit."

Coltrane turned to Alice. "You can ride behind me, Honey."

"If it's all right, Daddy, could I ride behind Bone on Hildebrandt?"

He looked over at Bone and raised his eyebrows.

Bone laughed. "Fine by me...he won't even know you're on there with me."

"I'll need help getting on."

"Oh, I don't think so."

They all walked over to where the horses were grazing. Bone saddled Hildebrandt, everyone else snugged their cinches up.

Hildebrandt did the same thing he did before—he knelt down on his front knees.

Alice grinned, stepped in the stirrup, and threw her leg over his back, behind the cantle. He nickered and stood back up.

Bone stuck his foot in the stirrup, lifted his leg over the saddlehorn and straddled the saddle in front of her. She wrapped her arms about his waist.

The others mounted and they splashed across the creek.

Bear Dog led out and crossed first.

The short mile to the camp passed quickly. They dismounted, ground-tied the horses, and looked at Coltrane.

"Need to make a couple of torches."

Bone shook his head. "Not necessary." He took his taclight from his *parfleche* and held it up. "Got a portable light from our time...Loraine has one, too."

"You're full of surprises."

Fiona smiled. "You don't know the half of it, Jip...Lead out."

"This way, folks." He grinned. "It was in the cave they stuck us in all along."

Bone nodded. "Hide in plain sight, huh?"

"Well, you could almost say that." He led everyone up the hill.

Bear Dog seemed to know where they were going as he padded on ahead straight to the cave.

They stood at the entrance.

"Bone, if you'll show me how to operate that device, I'll show ya'll that box."

"Here. Just push that button right there on the end."

Coltrane pushed it and the powerful beam of light extended out from the other end. "Amazin'."

Bone pointed inside. Coltrane headed into the interior, panning the light to show the way. As usual, Bear Dog went ahead.

They walked about fifty yards into the depths of the old silver mine. Around a turn in the shaft, they came to a pile of used boards and support timbers that covered a nook in the side wall.

"Bone, if you an' Mason will remove those boards an' timbers."

The two men quickly moved the covering to the side to reveal an old, tarnished, copper clad box.

"Drag it out here a ways."

He handed the taclight to Bone. "Shine it on the box."

Bear Dog sniffed of the box, then looked back at Bone and smiled.

Coltrane unhooked the three clasps across the front and grabbed the handle. He lifted the lid up as Bone shined the light on the contents.

Almost everyone gasped.

"There you have it, people...Eighty thousand dollars."

Bone chuckled and nodded. "In Confederate money."

Fiona looked at him. "Why didn't you just show them that what they wanted was worthless?"

"Knew that if I did...we were no longer necessary...an' dead witnesses don't talk."

Flynn nodded. "You were probably dead either way."

Coltrane glanced at Mason. "True."

§§§§§

PREVIEW

The Next Exciting Novel
From

KEN FARMER

COLTRANE

CHAPTER ONE

JACKSBORO, TEXAS

"Has the jury reached a verdict?"

The Forman got to his feet. "We have, your Honor."

"Will the defendant please stand and face the jury."

Coltrane got to his feet and turned to the jury.

The Forman looked at a paper in his hand, glanced at Jack County Judge Leonard Keeler, then at the defendant.

"We, the jury, find the defendant, James Coltrane, guilty of murder in the first degree."

There was a rumbling throughout the courtroom.

Bone got to his feet, but Loraine grabbed his arm and pulled him back down.

Alice Coltrane also stood. "No! No!"

Fiona Miller Flynn stood beside the teenager and hugged her.

Judge Keeler had a slight smile on his face as he nodded to the jury and turned to the defendant. "James Coltrane, a jury of your peers has found you guilty of the dastardly crime of murdering your wife, Alicia Coltrane, in the first degree. This court sentences you to hang by the neck until you are dead on the first day of December, the year of our Lord, 1902."

COLTRANE

Coltrane glared at the judge with eyes of burning steel. His stare was so intense, Judge Keeler was forced to look away.

He slammed his gavel. "Court dismissed."

The bailiff stood at the side of the courtroom. "All rise."

The black-robed, somewhat paunchy. fifty-year-old jurist with silver temples, and mutton-chop whiskers rapidly exited the Jack County courtroom to his chambers.

Bone, Loraine, Fiona, and Mason Flynn gathered at the back of the courtroom as everyone exited.

Bone shook his head. "Well, so much for facts."

"They just didn't understand about rigor mortis, Bone."

"I know, Fiona. Looked to me like the jurors were all scared to death of that judge."

Loraine shook her head. "I just don't understand why. The facts were plain as day."

"Remember what you said about Democrats, Babe?"

"I know, but I was halfway joking...then."

Alice's jaw muscles flexed as she watched the guards escort her father from the courtroom.

He turned his head, blew a kiss to her, and winked.

"There's no way I'm going to let them hang my father." The look in her eyes matched that of Jip Coltrane's.

Fiona put her arm around the fifteen-year-old again. "We'll file an appeal with the District Court in Wichita Falls, Alice...That will at least give us some time."

Alice shook her head. "I just don't trust 'em...any of 'em. There's too much of that legal double-talk and rigmarole...Like listenin' to a bunch of monkeys jabbering."

Bone turned to Loraine. "She learns quick."

Alice looked at the big man. "Not hard when it's obvious they're crooked as a bucket of fish hooks."

The sun settled beneath the western horizon and darkness crept toward Jacksboro from the east. The gloaming, halfway between day and night, engulfed the north Texas area as the stars winked into view.

Deputy Platt got to his feet from behind his desk in the Jack County Sheriff's office. He opened the door to the cell area.

"Hey, Jip, gonna run over to Ruth Ann's an' git yer supper. Be back in a little bit."

"That's fine, Harlan, not plannin' on goin' anywhere."

The longtime deputy grinned, turned, headed out the front door and locked it behind him.

Harlan Platt had been Jip Coltrane's chief deputy since the election to replace Mason Flynn three years earlier.

Jip laid down on his bunk, clasped his hands behind his head, and stared at the plaster ceiling.

He turned his head and looked at the thick back door as it 'clicked' and swung open.

A figure in a tan canvas jacket, blue jeans, boots, and a brown Huck Finn hat stepped though from the twilight outside.

Jip jumped to his feet as the figure approached the cell. He looked into the gray eyes of his daughter, her long blonde tresses were tucked up under her hat. Her outfit gave her all the outward appearance of a teenage boy.

"Alice! What are you doin' here?"

"Getting you, that's what."

"You can't do that! It's jail breakin'."

"And you know it doesn't do any good to argue with me...I'm just like mama was. My mind's made up, Daddy. You don't have a chance while you're in here...be right back."

"But..."

Alice disappeared into the front office and came back quickly. She inserted the brass jail door key into the large inset lock on the iron barred door.

It grated a little as it unlocked—she pulled the door open and handed him his gunbelt and ivory-handled Colt .45 she'd draped over her shoulder. "Here's your gun."

"Honey..."

Alice wagged her finger at him. "Uh-uh, no time. Got Red saddled outside. We have to hurry. Harlan will be back soon."

"Oh, Lord." He buckled the gunbelt around his waist. "Where'd you get the key to the back door?"

She looked a little askance at him. "Daddy, you've been sheriff here for three years. You always leave your key ring on your dresser in your bedroom."

"Oh, right."

She locked the cell door behind him after he stepped out into the hallway.

"Be right back." She went back into the front office to return the cell door key to Harlan's desk and closed the door behind her.

"Why did you lock the cell door back an' replace the key?"

"Simple, to create a little confusion. He'll see you're gone when he brings your supper from Ruth Ann's. All the doors will be locked, but you've vanished...Poof."

"You're about half dangerous, you know that?"

She winked at him. "Just half?...Let's go. The horses are waiting."

"You're not goin'."

She gave him her look again.

"Oh, my Lord in Heaven."

He followed her out the door to where Red and her dun gelding, Buttercup, were tied.

"Let's ride."

COLTRANE

He rolled his eyes at her as they mounted and trotted the horses out of town to the west.

Deputy Platt entered the Sheriff's office carrying a covered tray and set it on his desk. He got the key from the top drawer, picked the tray back up, braced it on his hip, and opened the door to the cell area.

"Light a lamp soon's I give you yer dinner, Jip...Ruth Ann fixed you fried chicken, mashed taters, biscuits an' gravy plus apple pie on 'count she knows it's yer favorite." He stepped to the cell, braced the tray on his hip again and stuck the key in the door.

"Here you go, Sheriff." He looked into the dimly lit cell before he turned the key. "Jip?...Jip?...What the Sam Hill?" He bent over and peered underneath the bunk.

Deputy Platt set the tray on the floor, tugged on the door. "Locked." He walked to the back door and twisted the knob.

"Locked." He turned around with a panicked look.

JUDGE LEONARD KEELER'S OFFICE

The bright November sun shown through the windows of the judge's office. A knock sounded on the door to his inner sanctum.

"Enter."

His secretary, Maude, a dowdy fifty-year-old woman with mousy brown hair up in a tight bun, flecked with gray, opened the door.

"Deputy Platt to see you, Sir."

"Send him in."

He reached over to his humidor, removed a dark Virginia cigar, bit the ends off as the deputy entered and stood in front of his desk, twisting his worn Bollman Heritage bowler around in his hands.

Keeler picked up a rather clunky German Döbereiner lighter and lit the end. He exhaled a blue cloud of smoke over his head, leaned back, and then looked at Platt.

"What is it?"

"Uh...Judge, uh...ain't real sure how this happened...but..."

"But what, man? Get to it! Don't have all day."

"Well...Sir, seems like Sheriff Coltrane disappeared yest'dy evenin' while I wus gittin' his supper..."

Keeler shot to his feet, dropping his cigar to his desktop. "What are you saying, man?"

"He's gone, Sir, like a ghost er somethin'. All the doors wus still locked, cell included...He wus just gone. Looked all over an'...nothin'."

The color drained from Judge Keeler's face as he collapsed back into his padded leather chair.

§§§

AUTHOR

Ken Farmer didn't write his first full novel until he was sixty-nine years of age. He often wonders what the hell took him so long. At age eighty-one...he is currently working on novel number forty-eight.

Ken spent thirty years raising cattle and quarter horses in Texas and forty-five years as a professional actor. Those years gave him a background for storytelling...or as he has been known to say, "I've always been a bit of a bull---t artist, writing novels kind of came naturally once it occurred to me I could put my stories down on paper."

His favorite expression is: "Just tell the damn story."

Writing has become Ken's second life: he has been a Marine, played collegiate football, been a Texas wildcatter, cattle and horse rancher, professional film and TV actor and director, and now...a novelist. Who knew?

Ken Farmer's dialogue flows like a beautiful western river...it's the gold standard...Carole Beers

OTHER NOVELS FROM
TIMBER CREEK PRESS

MILITARY ACTION/TECHNO
BLACK EAGLE FORCE: Eye of the Storm (Book #1)
by Buck Stienke and Ken Farmer
BLACK EAGLE FORCE: Sacred Mountain (Book #2) by Buck Stienke and Ken Farmer
RETURN of the STARFIGHTER (Book #3)
by Buck Stienke and Ken Farmer
BLACK EAGLE FORCE: BLOOD IVORY (Book #4) by Buck Stienke and Ken Farmer with Doran Ingrham
BLACK EAGLE FORCE: FOURTH REICH (Book #5) by Buck Stienke and Ken Farmer
AURORA: INVASION (Book #6 in the BEF) by Ken Farmer & Buck Stienke
BLACK EAGLE FORCE: ISIS (Book #7) by Buck Stienke and Ken Farmer
BLOOD BROTHERS - Doran Ingrham, Buck Stienke and Ken Farmer
DARK SECRET - Doran Ingrham
NICARAGUAN HELL - Doran Ingrham

HISTORICAL FICTION WESTERN
THE NATIONS by Ken Farmer and Buck Stienke

HAUNTED FALLS by Ken Farmer and Buck Stienke

HELL HOLE by Ken Farmer

ACROSS the RED by Ken Farmer and Buck Stienke

BASS and the LADY by Ken Farmer and Buck Stienke

DEVIL'S CANYON by Buck Stienke

LADY LAW by Ken Farmer

BLUE WATER WOMAN by Ken Farmer

FLYNN by Ken Farmer

AURALI RED by Ken Farmer

COLDIRON by Ken Farmer

STEELDUST by Ken Farmer

BONE by Ken Farmer

BONE'S LAW by Ken Farmer

BONE & LORAINE by Ken Farmer

BONE'S GOLD by Ken Farmer

BONE'S ENIGMA by Ken Farmer

SILKE JUSTICE by Ken Farmer

SILKE'S QUEST by Ken Farmer

NO TIME to DIE by Buck Stienke

SILKE'S RIDE by Ken Farmer

ANGEL JUSTICE by Ken Farmer

SKINWALKER JUSTICE by Ken Farmer

DALIA MARRH by Ken Farmer

THE RETURN by Ken Farmer

RED CANYON by Ken Farmer
HILDEBRANDT & BEAR DOG by Ken Farmer

COMING SOON
COLTRANE by Ken Farmer

SY/FY
LEGEND of AURORA by Ken Farmer & Buck Stienke
AURORA: INVASION (Book #6 in the BEF) by Ken Farmer & Buck Stienke

MYSTERY
BONE'S PARADOX by Buck Stienke
RECIPE for MURDER by Ken Farmer & Buck Stienke
SIN NO MORE by Ken Farmer & Buck Stienke
THE LOCK BOX by Terry D. Heflin

AWARD-WINNING THREE CREEKS MYSTERY SERIES
THREE CREEKS by Ken Farmer
RED HILL ROAD by Ken Farmer
THE POND by Ken Farmer
UNION COUNTY by Ken Farmer
KILGORE by Ken Farmer
OLD DOGS an' OLD ROADS by Ken Farmer

POSSUM HOLLAR by Ken Farmer
SPIRIT TREE by Ken Farmer

CIVIL WAR ESPIONAGE ROMANCE
SCARLET HEM by Terry D. Heflin
GOLDEN CIRCLE by Terry D. Heflin
THE AMETHYST by Terry D. Heflin

COMING SOON
FOUR ACES by Terry D. Heflin

HISTORICAL FICTION ROMANCE
THE TEMPLAR TRILOGY
MYSTERIOUS TEMPLAR by Adriana Girolami
THE CRIMSON AMULET by Adriana Girolami
TEMPLAR'S REDEMPTION by Adriana Girolami
THE ZAMINDAR'S BRIDE by Adriana Girolami

COMING SOON
DAUGHTER of HADES by Adriana Girolami

TIMBER CREEK PRESS

Made in the USA
Middletown, DE
11 December 2022